DEATH AT CLOSE QUARTERS

The brave that Leach hadn't hit appeared from the front side of the wagon directly to his left. He must've been hiding, waiting for the right moment to make his move and figured this was it. He lunged at me and likely would have killed me had his knife not caught itself in the side of the big buckskin jacket I wore and carried my shells in. As it was he only tore the pocket some. By the time he'd recovered his knife and his balance, so had I. I'd also swung my Spencer around by then and pulled the trigger. The force of the .52-caliber bullet and charge was a heavy one . . . .

SPENCER'S REVENGE

Jim Miller

FAWCETT GOLD MEDAL • NEW YORK

A Fawcett Gold Medal Book
Published by Ballantine Books
Copyright © 1987 by James L. Collins

Library of Congress Catalog Card Number: 86-91369

ISBN 0-449-13059-2

Manufactured in the United States of America

First Edition: March 1987

This one's for Mary Hood, for believing in me. Now *that's* friendship!

Chapter 1

I took aim on him real careful like, figuring if I took him out of this game we might have a better chance. I had him right in the sights of my Spencer, just like Pa showed us, and was squeezing the trigger as he rode by, when my hat went flying off. Actually, my hat went flying off about the same time that Cheyenne war chief became a feather duster. But that didn't stop the cold chill from running down my spine, knowing that I'd just come one step shy of dying myself.

"By God, there might be room for you in this land yet, Hooker!" Even being under siege by a band of Indians like we were, I could still hear the booming voice of Leach, the big, overbearing wagon master of the supposed wagon train we were leading to Denver.

What I wasn't prepared for was the forceful slap on the back this bear of a man gave me. It threw me forward into the side of the wagon, scaring the horses. Leach thought he was being friendly by doing it, but right then I wasn't in the mood for his kind of friendship.

"Damn it, Leach, don't do that." I gave him a quick, hard glance as I reloaded my Spencer rifle. My hat was on the ground, where the arrow had carried it off my head.

1

Again a shiver went through me. I hardly noticed it when the wagon master returned my glare, for the Cheyenne were making another pass at us.

But we were ready for them, and the dozen or so men in our small wagon train managed to shoot about six or seven of the war party that was making a go at us. Leach went over to another wagon for more ammunition and I took a chance and climbed up on the driver's box of the one I'd been behind to look inside.

"You all right, Miss Botkin?" I asked.

"Yes, Diah," she replied, then, as if realizing she'd made a mistake, added, "I mean, Mister Hooker." I thought I saw the curve of a tiny smile start at the corner of her mouth as she said it.

"Long as you're not harmed, ma'am," I said, about to bring a hand up to tip my hat and suddenly realizing how foolish I must have looked doing it.

A shot rang out and I jumped down from the wagon seat, hoping the girl inside had the common sense to take cover as well. Some of the Indians on the plains had taken repeaters and revolvers off those they'd killed, so it was hard to tell who was doing the shooting sometimes. As it turned out, it was one of our men who'd fired. Still, this was no time to be throwing caution to the wind, no matter how pretty a girl looked. And Rebecca Botkin was the prettiest girl I'd ever seen.

"We're thinning 'em out, lads," Leach bellowed, although I thought I detected a note of despair in his voice. "Just make sure you make every shot count. We don't want to run low on ammunition. Got it?" There was some muttering among the men as they took to checking their powder and ball.

I may have been only eighteen, but I'd been doing a man's work for a long time already, and that makes you learn things right quick. And I'd learned years before to see what I was looking at and listen proper to what I was hearing. Between the look on Leach's face and a tone in his voice that just didn't ring true, I knew we were in trouble.

"How much ammunition have you got for that fancy rifle of yours?" he asked as he neared me.

"You're running low on ammunition, aren't you?" was all I said, staring dead into his eyes, looking for what I was sure the others hadn't spotted. And I was right. Leach was the kind of man who'd never admit he was scared to death for fear he'd be laughed at and lose respect. Pa taught us boys different. Me, you bet I was scared, but I also figured I'd live to tell about it.

"I asked how much ammunition you had, you young—" he started to growl, the meanness in him showing again.

"I've got twenty-eight rounds left for my Spencer, plus whatever's in the rifle now and a full round in my Colt." I said it low and even, the look on my face telling him he was pushing it. "You want to try finishing that sentence after we get through with this fight, Leach, you go right ahead. First we gotta get out of this fracas." He'd tried bullying me before, being nearly twice my age, but I'd not taken it from him, not at all. Like I said, Pa taught us a lot. "What happened to Prather?" I asked when he stayed silent. "I thought you said he was a good sharp-shooter."

"He *was*. He's dead," Leach said, the worry in him now even more evident. "Red devils got him from the side and made off with a case of our ammunition."

In a way I could see how that kind of news might panic these folks. Not all of them were as used to the land as Leach and I were, and there was more than enough fear to go around right now anyway.

"Here they come!" someone yelled out. It was all the

warning any of us needed. I reckon instinct sort of takes over when it comes to surviving in this land, and as long as you can keep a steady trigger finger and a loaded weapon around you—well, you might have a chance. But I'll tell you, hoss, those Cheyenne looked more fearsome with each charge they made at us. I had a feeling I knew what Pa had been talking about when he said that warring aged you something fierce, no matter what your born age was.

We'd thinned them out all right, Leach was right about that. When they first hit us, I'd have sworn they were at least sixty or seventy in number. They'd made two charges at us so far, and now they looked to number thirty-five at most as they came at us again. But in the few seconds it took for them to get into range I did some adding and subtracting and came away with a notion that maybe we hadn't done in as many as we believed.

Or else that's what they wanted us to think!

An arrow struck the side of the wagon at the same time our enemy to the front also became our enemy to the rear. I turned to see half a dozen or more Indians rushing toward us, and watched one brave's arrow plunge into the back of one of our men.

"Never mind these sonsabitches!" Leach yelled above the gunfire and the screaming. "Get the front! Get the front!"

The big man was making himself a target for any one of those warriors who wanted a piece of him, and as much as I didn't like him personally, I can't say that I could fault his accuracy with a pistol—or two for that matter, which was what he had. Something had grazed him, an arrow or bullet, but he simply stood straight like there was no tomorrow and made sure that there would be none for those sneaky devils. The rest of us dropped a few more as they rode across our front, but were surprised when they didn't turn and charge again.

"The wagon! They got the damn wagon!" Once again it was Leach yelling above the noise that surrounded us all. Two of the braves who'd survived his gunfire had jumped up on a wagon we all knew carried the rest of our ammunition. If it was taken we'd have no ammunition at all, including what I used for my Spencer!

I ran to an opening where I could see the two braves, who'd now taken the reins in their hands and were riding off with the wagon. I levered another round into my rifle, cocked it, quickly took aim, and shot one of them out of the seat at seventy-five yards. Gathering up the reins of a free mount, I noticed that aside from a few shots here and there, the air was filled with relative silence compared to only a few minutes ago. But I knew my share of the fighting wasn't over yet today, not by a long shot!

Once mounted, I slipped a fresh tube of ammunition from my pocket into the butt of the Spencer, making sure I had enough to do me for a ride after that wagon. Outside the camp it seemed as though the Indians had disappeared; crawled into the scenery just as quickly as they'd come from it. The scary thought that they were now waiting up ahead to join that wagonload of ammunition I was chasing didn't help my confidence. Still, I put heels to the horse and ran him as hard and fast as I could, pulling up alongside the driver's box and pulling the trigger on my rifle as soon as I could bring it to bear on the lone Cheyenne now holding the reins. The slug pierced his side, likely going through his lungs and heart, and he fell into the boot, the reins slipping from his hands.

The team wasn't made for running flat out, and soon slowed to a halt. I got rid of the Indian and headed the wagon and its precious supplies back to camp.

I was right about the remaining Cheyenne fading away, but they'd done it for a different reason than I'd suspected. As I drove the wagon back into camp, I saw a dozen heav-

ily armed men ride up from the opposite direction. Unless
I missed my guess, they would be the reason the war party
had fled. The renegade Indians might have outnumbered
the whites, but the braves also knew they'd be going up
against repeaters if they took the newcomers on. Against
Colts, Henrys, Spencers and a variety of other such rifles
and pistols, a bow and arrow were no match.

The men who'd saved the day claimed to belong to a
group called the Colorado Third Volunteers. They'd heard
the massive gunfire and had come a-running just in time to
keep us from taking any more losses than we did. Leach
invited them to stay the night, for we had only one more
day of travel before we'd reach Denver, and no one protested.

The look of gratitude those in our wagon train had for
our saviors wasn't nearly as surprising as the reception I
got when I returned with the wagonload of ammunition. I
was no sooner down off the box than Rebecca Botkin came
flying into my arms and kissed me to boot! Now, don't get
me wrong, I liked her. Hell, I liked her a lot! But what she
did . . . why, you just didn't do that in public! So I pushed
her away, slowly feeling the back of my neck turn about
as red as any wound.

"Ma'am, you hadn't oughtta . . . I mean—"

"But you saved it, Diah!" she said, pleased as punch.
"You saved the wagon and—"

"Don't be fussing about it," Leach said, stepping forward. "He's getting paid to scout and fight. You just get
back to the other women and fix us up some vittles."

For a second there I'd had a feeling about Becky, one
that hadn't crossed my mind before, but once and then only
fleetingly. I'd felt something for her I'd never felt before
for anyone, but I couldn't place it, couldn't put my finger
on it. Maybe that's why I paid more attention to her as she
walked away that afternoon.

* * *

Samuel Botkin, Becky's father, had used that fancy telegraph they'd strung up to get hold of me at Fort Kearney. He'd been in Denver since the start of the place back in '59 and was a friend to Pa. Ezra Hooker, that's my pa's name. Some call him Black Jack, but those are mostly folks he considers friends and you'd better believe that *those* are few and far between. But like Pa says, that's a whole 'nother canyon. Anyway, Mister Botkin had gotten hold of me by this new telegraph device they had, asking if I would escort his daughter out to Denver. He gave me Leach's name as the wagon master and said he'd leave word at Fort Riley that I would meet up with the wagon train there and scout for the train and escort his daughter all in one. He was offering me a hundred dollars if I'd do it, so I wired him back saying I would. Hell, that was three months' pay and more for maybe one month's work, and you didn't often come by wages like that out here.

But I knew I'd be earning every last cent of it. Nearly everyone on the Kansas plains knew that Denver was all but shut off from civilization and supplies by the Arapahoe and Cheyenne who'd taken to the warpath again. It seemed to be a yearly occurrence since the War Between the States had started. Damn near every Union soldier had been pulled off the plains and sent back east to fight the war, so the Indians had taken advantage of it and went on the warpath during the spring, summer, and fall months, then sued for peace so they could live on the reservation during the winter and get fed by the same government they'd go back to warring against the next spring. But it was the fall of 1864 now, and things had been worse this year between the frontiersmen and the Indians. A whole lot worse.

I had no doubt that word of the Hungate Massacre had reached back even as far as St. Louis and Fort Leavenworth, where most of the wagon trains began. The Hungate family had been massacred by the renegades on the war-path back in June. Now, friend, fighting for your life out here gets to be a way of life, so you come to expect such things as what happened to the Hungates. But when the bodies were taken to Denver and put on public display . . . why, even the governor of the Colorado Territory got rattled at the sight of such mutilation.

That was why I called this group a "supposed" wagon train, for there were only eight wagons to it, along with a supply wagon and the ammunition. Oh, there were plenty of folks who wanted to come west to the strikes in and around Denver, but only seven families had had the courage to carry out that desire. They were the ones Rebecca Botkin had joined up with in order to get to Denver to be with her father. They either didn't know that there was one hell of a war building up out here on the plains, or they didn't care, one or the other. And to tell the truth, even after the close call we'd just had, I found myself glad that Samuel Botkin had wanted me to escort his daughter to Denver for him.

"You've got a nice way of smiling, Diah."

It was later that night, when the fires were dying down and I'd walked off by myself just to do some thinking. She caught me by surprise, and if it were anyone else, I'd have read to them from the book, but I found her presence a pleasant one, surprise or not.

"Here," she said, offering me a cup of coffee, "this is the last of it. Thought you might like it."

The sun was about to set and it was getting dark. I took the cup. And I took her in.

"What're you staring at?" She had a soft, easy way of talking that made a body want to open up to her, and I couldn't but hope that one day I'd have the courage to do that.

"Nothing." I smiled back at her, taking a swallow of

the lukewarm liquid. There wasn't much light, but I'll tell you something, hoss, we could've been in the darkest of caves and I wouldn't have had to look at her at all to know what Rebecca Botkin looked like. Long black hair with eyes that matched; they had caution to them at first, but after I'd seen her a few times, the wariness was gone and now there was a longing in them. She had high cheekbones that favored the dark-tanned skin that wasn't tanned at all. She was slim but taller than most women, and she carried herself with pride. Those who were new to the land would have to look twice, maybe three times to confirm their suspicions, but I was born out here and I knew right off, just like Leach likely had. And it didn't matter at all to me that she was a half-breed. Her being Rebecca Botkin was enough.

"What you did today was very brave." Slowly, softly, she placed a hand on each side of my face, as though to hold it still while she kissed my lips. When we parted, there was still enough light to see a twinkle in her eye, one of delight in what she had just done. "I meant it this afternoon and I mean it now." She took the cup from me, knowing the contents were now cold, and poured it out. "I like you, Mister Jedediah Hooker." What I had thought to be a smile turned out to be just that, her teeth white in the darkness. "Yes, I do."

Then she was gone.

I watched her go, more appreciative of her now than before, glad that I had met her when I did. She made me feel good inside, and in the world I lived, that seemed a rarity indeed. I knew that I would see her again, knew it was not over between us. But watching her go, I also had an uneasy feeling. It was the kind you pick up in the Chiricahua Mountains when you pass through them, knowing that likely as not an Apache is watching your every move.

Chapter 2

We made it to Denver without further incident.

Denver was turning out to be just like the mining cities of the California Gold Rush days, the only difference being that it didn't have the Pacific Ocean just to its west. Instead, it had one hell of a big mountain range that Pa had been telling me about ever since I was a youngster. The Rocky Mountains some called them, although those who'd lived there like Pa and the other mountain men referred to them as the "Shinin' Mountains." You could see their snow-capped peaks more than a day away from Denver, and even at that distance you'd know what those old-timers were meaning by "shinin' " mountains.

Other than that . . . well, like I said, Denver hadn't turned out to be much different than some of those big-time cities in California, even after five or so years of prosperity. Some of the buildings had become permanent in structure, but there were still a lot with false fronts and less than cordial interiors that you wouldn't want to take a lady to. Which was why most of those establishments didn't allow women in them unless they worked there, and those women didn't have much to speak of in the way of reputation. In the summer the streets were dirt; the rest of the year they were usually a quagmire of mud and rain.

"Nothing paved like them fancy back-east cities," I said to Becky as we entered Denver, breaking away from the rest of the wagon train, "but at least you didn't get here real early in the spring or later in the fall, toward winter time."

"I'm not complaining," she said, "as long as I can be with Papa." She smiled in a pleasing way as she spoke and, as I'd been doing all day long, I'd felt a rush of blood creeping up my neck.

"Yes, ma'am." I found myself losing my voice when I wanted to keep it most.

I hadn't seen Samuel Botkin in at least a year, but he hadn't changed in that time. He was of average height, balding somewhat, but as muscular in build and jovial in nature as I'd remembered him. Pa had met Samuel Botkin when he'd come back to Denver from someplace in Kansas—Lawrence I think he said it was—to do some healing. Pa had been tracking down some killers, a purely family matter, you understand, and had gotten shot up. He couldn't stop talking about some fellow who'd helped him by the name of Hickok or Barnes, I forget which. Listening to him talk, I had the notion that Pa didn't much like this Hickok character but still had a good healthy respect for him. And as the story unfolded, it was clear that this other fellow'd had that same kind of grudging respect for Pa. But that was Black Jack Hooker for you.

"Rebecca!" To say that Samuel Botkin was excited about the arrival of his daughter would be an understatement. He was standing right out in front of the general store he ran and, spotting Rebecca, all but yanked her off the driver's box with as much energy as had been displayed by the warriors we'd encountered only a short ways from Denver.

"I'll get the wagon," I said, but they didn't hear me, too busy embracing one another with bear hugs, both talking at once as they did so. Actually, I felt sort of let down, left like that after all of the attention she'd given me of late, but it was her father whose arms she was in now and I tried to understand it as best I could. Once I had put the wagon around back, I entered his store, and saw the two of them still exchanging news with each other, still excited about seeing each other again.

"Well, now," Mister Botkin said, finally noticing me in the doorway, "you *have* filled out, haven't you?" He smiled and stuck a beefy hand out. "Thanks, Jedediah. Your pa said I could rely on you to get Becky here safely."

"That almost didn't come about," I replied, taking his hand. "Pa still down south with Carson's volunteers?" He nodded. Kit Carson and his New Mexico Volunteers had been fighting Indians and Rebels for nearly three years now, and Pa had mentioned something about heading back to Old Taos the last time I'd seen him. When Samuel Botkin had wired to ask me to escort his daughter out here to Denver, he'd made mention that Pa was still away.

"Becky, do you know that the last time I saw this boy . . . why, he was a couple of inches shorter and a mite skinnier—"

"Papa, please," she said, blushing.

"Now look at him," he said with the same measure of pride that Pa would've used, "taller'n me and . . ." The sentence trailed off as he stood back, taking in my appearance like one of those army sergeants does that of a new recruit. "Damn, but you growed some, boy!"

He was right. I had filled out quite a bit in the last year or two. It wasn't the hard work or long hours, I don't think, as much as it was being my time for it. A tree doesn't grow much differently than a human does. Both start out small but tend to grow fast before stopping for a while.

Then you think they'll never grow anymore and quick as you turn around they have. And most times they turn out better than you expect them to. Both my pa and my older brother were taller than me, but I stood an inch or two over six foot, and in this land that was considered to be big.

"Some, Mister Botkin," I smiled shyly, "just some."

"You call me Samuel, Jedediah. Or Sam, just like your pa does." The front door opened then and some customers came in. "You two stay right here. Let me take care of these people."

"Papa talks a blue streak," Rebecca said, a slight blush coming to her cheeks as she watched the older man walk to the front of the store.

"I'll say. Why, last year I sat all night without saying one single word while your pa and mine tried to see who could out-lie the other." Whether she heard me or not I don't know, for she had eyes only for Samuel Botkin now. A smile came to her lips as she watched him.

"You've got a right fine smile, ma'am," I said. Maybe it was my formality that startled her. When she turned back to me, she wore a curious frown that quickly returned to that pleasant smile I'd just seen.

"No. You must call me Becky." It was clear it was me she was noticing now. "The Diah is from Jedediah?"

"Yes, ma'am . . . uh, Becky," I corrected her hastily. "Only thing Ma ever got Pa to agree to do was give us boys names out of the Bible."

"Somehow, I've a notion your name didn't exactly come from the Good Book," she said, thoroughly enjoying herself now. Me, I may have been the one she was funning, but I sort of enjoyed it my own self, to be honest.

"Don't you bother none about him at all, woman." I didn't have to look further than the entrance of the store to know who the gravelly voice belonged to, for Leach always made his presence known, no matter where he went.

"He done his job and he's moving on, pronto. Ain't that right, pilgrim?" The last was an out-and-out threat from the tone of his voice and the look of his face, no doubt about that. "Gonna take you to some of the finer places in this town." It was as much an order as any he'd made the previous day during the Indian attack. "Yes, ma'am. Gonna take you myself. Right now."

Rebecca gave me a confused, angry look, obviously not sure what was going on. Now, friend, I wasn't either, but you can bet that when Leach got close enough to take hold of her arm, I had the business end of that Spencer stuck into his midsection. It stopped him dead cold. The silence that followed gave me just enough time to let everyone hear the loud cocking noise my rifle can make. And with the barrel stuck in your gut, well, mister, I can guarantee you'll be a believer real quick if you ain't already.

"You're dumber than I figured, Leach," I said as though we were having a normal conversation. But there wasn't nothing normal happening right then and we all knew it. "I thought you'd learned by now that you can't bully me."

"You won't get away with this, you little—"

"Still pushing that around, are you?" I hadn't moved, but the big man had let go of Becky's arm and was concentrating fully on me now.

"Looks to me like he is." I didn't know which one of us Samuel Botkin was talking to or about, but he'd all of a sudden decided to take a hand in this game. He still had his store apron on, but the sleeves of his shirt were rolled high enough to expose thick, muscular forearms that had gotten that way only by moving many a case of supplies.

"Maybe you didn't notice the sign out front, my friend, but it says BOTKIN'S GENERAL STORE. Well, I'm Samuel Botkin, and that means I own it." He wasn't what you think of as your typical storekeeper right now. More like an angry father, only I wasn't sure Leach was aware of the relationship between the man and woman before him. But he was going to find out damn soon. Sooner than I thought, for he made one hell of a mistake right then, Leach did.

"That don't make this none of your affair," Leach said in his meanest voice. "This girl ain't nothing but—"

He never finished it. Never had the chance to. I met one of those fancy educated fellows from back east one time, the kind that always carries around his Webster's to make sure he's using the right words. If he fished around in his big word book, he'd likely come up with ambidextrous to describe Samuel Botkin, but to me he was plain two-fisted. You see, the storekeeper had thrown a hard left cross that snapped Leach's face to the side and sent him staggering to the rear. And while he was recovering from the sting of it, Botkin used his other hand to pull out the man's pistol and was now nudging the barrel just under Leach's throat, an action that made the big man's eyes bulge with fear.

"My *daughter* is what she is," he hissed, "and if any other word besides that one ever comes out of your mouth to describe her . . . well, they won't call you my *friend* anymore. Just dead. That's what they'll call you."

Tears began to well up in Rebecca's eyes, but I wasn't sure I knew why. I never was much good at figuring women out. Most of us Hooker men aren't. All I knew was that what had happened here shouldn't have and I was feeling the same mad that Samuel Botkin had in him now.

"If I was you, Leach, I'd make myself scarce around this store," I said.

"That's right," Botkin added, "you're probably giving me a bad reputation right now."

He escorted the big man to the front door, but when Leach put out his hand for his pistol, Samuel just tossed it carelessly out into the dusty street, with a look that dared the man to do or say anything else to him.

He didn't.

Botkin quickly took care of the customers who had stayed to watch the confrontation—and would likely spread the story around like wildfire now in every version but the truth—and was soon at his daughter's side.

"Oh, Papa," I heard her say in a muffled voice as she hid her face in Samuel Botkin's chest. "It's going to start all over again, all over again."

"No, it's not, damn it!" Her words had sparked something in him, a memory, I thought, that brought out one hell of a lot of determination on his part. He had her by the shoulders now, at arm's length, talking to her like she was a little girl again. "You start life only once, Becky, and that's when you're born. Everything that happens between then and the time you die just . . . happens." He shrugged and I saw the love of a father for his daughter in his eyes, much the same as I'd remembered Pa looking at me from time to time in my own youth. He took her in his arms then and she held on for dear life, just like a little nine-year-old girl would to her daddy, only Rebecca Botkin was close to my age. The man's voice softened considerably as he said, "You're just getting used to a new place that, unfortunately, has a set way of thinking about those who live in it." He held her silently for a while, then thrust her out at arm's length again, but with a smile on his face this time.

"I have two questions," he said, glancing from his daughter to me. "First," he said, addressing her, "can you cook any better than when I left you with Aunt Louise?"

"Yes, Papa," she said, her face filled with pleasure and happiness now. "Much better."

To me he said, "And how would you feel about joining the Botkin family for supper, young man?"

"Well, I—"

"Yes," Rebecca said, glancing my way with a smile. "Yes, he will be there, Papa."

Samuel Botkin gave me a mock look of defeat as he raised his eyebrows. "I'm told they've been this way since time immemorial. Talk about food or mention a kitchen and a man is likely to find out who the *real* boss in the family is."

Rebecca blushed, then laughed.

As I recall, I laughed with her.

Chapter 3

"I've heard a lot about that Spencer," Samuel Botkin said to me about an hour later as I sat at a corner table of his store, cleaning my weapons and trying to stay out of the way as much as possible. It was nearing closing time now and business had slacked off. "Sell a helluva lot of ammunition for it, I know that."

"From what I hear, President Lincoln test-fired it himself and made it the official rifle of the Union Army," I said, adding a touch of oil here and there. "Yes, sir, it has gotten pretty popular."

The Spencer carbine and rifle weren't all that new to the west. The War Between the States had been going on for a long time now, but it had been back in 1860 that Christopher Spencer had gotten himself a patent for a repeating rifle and carbine that soon bore his name. The breechlock of the weapon was operated by the trigger guard acting as a lever, a principle not unlike that employed by the Sharps. When the lever was swung down, the breech opened, ejecting the spent cartridge and bringing a new load into the barrel. It was how those additional rounds were loaded that sort of threw you at first. Pa had a Henry repeater that sported a tubular magazine under the barrel. But now my

Spencer. Oh, it had a tubular magazine all right, but it was contained in the stock of the rifle. The magazine of a Spencer held only half the number of rounds that Pa's Henry did, but I'd become proficient enough with the rifle to be able to load and fire two of the seven-round tubular magazines in one minute's time, which was as good as Pa could with his Henry any day. You had to hand-cock the hammer on the weapon, but it was still one of the fastest-firing repeaters of its day. Yes, sir, the Spencer was a mighty popular gun about then.

"That right?" the storekeeper said after I'd explained to him what I knew about the weapon. "How's it on range?"

"Fair to middlin', I'd say." I finished checking the loads of my magazines. "The Sharps and Pa's Henry and a Hawken will likely outdo it when it comes to distance shots, Samuel, but I've a feeling that being effective during close-in fighting is what Mister Lincoln had in mind when he picked the Spencer for a saddle gun for his soldiers. That's where most of the fighting in that back-east war is being done anyway, I understand—at close range."

"True." I had Samuel Botkin's interest now; had him wondering about the rifle I carried as if it was part of me. "But what about out here? It seems to me you boys went through a fair amount of fighting to get Becky into Denver."

I smiled at him, knowing that what I'd say was the same any other man would who'd fought Indians on the plains. "Well, sir, I reckon you could say that when it comes to Indians, we just let 'em get close enough to start collecting lead." When a somewhat confused and concerned look crossed his face, I added, "Like Pa says, Samuel, I'm the one telling the story." He smiled then, and Becky called us to supper.

The side beef and spuds we ate were nothing out of the ordinary, but the biscuits Becky had made added a special taste to what might otherwise have been normal fare for a citified frontier meal. She made damn good coffee, too, and I made a point of telling her that.

"Oh, it's nothing," she said, pouring another cup and blushing at the same time. In the time I'd known her I'd discovered that she had a habit of not taking credit when she was due it.

"You're dead wrong, Rebecca," I said as she walked away. It was a statement that stopped her cold in her tracks, and she slowly turned back to face me. One other thing I'd found out about her was that she could be right feisty when she wanted to.

A frown came to her face, a challenge, actually, that told me she wasn't used to being talked to like that. "Really," was all she said, throwing me a cold, hard look out of the corner of her eye as she replaced the coffeepot on the table with a bang.

"Yes, ma'am." If that's the way she wanted it, then so be it. "Trouble is, there's some men out here that can shoot a flea off'n a grizzly at five hundred yards, and that's saying something, ma'am, it surely is."

"And?" She still had that stiff look about her; acting as though she'd been insulted in some way. Hell, maybe she had, I didn't know.

"But they can't make coffee worth spit," her father interjected, likely seeing what was coming in this confrontation. "I don't know what your recipe is, darlin', but I want it. By God, Jedediah's right! You do make the best coffee I've ever tasted!"

Hearing her father say it must've been what made it all right, but there was the kind of silence that you feel before a dawn attack during the rest of that meal. Awkward was the only way to describe how I felt, sitting there. When I was through, I said the proper thank-yous and walked out the back of the store.

The sun had about set, and night and the peaceful sort of silence that comes with it took over as the stars appeared. I could hear the distant nighttime movements of the city that I still hadn't become used to—saloons crowded with hard-drinking men, an occasional wagon or rider slowly going down the main street. It was sounds like that that disturbed me, making me as cautious about city folk as my pa and my brother were.

"I'll take the plains any day," I said softly to no one in particular.

"So would I," came a voice from behind me. By the time I'd turned to see it was Rebecca, I had my Spencer in hand, about to do battle. "Please," she said, taking a cautious step back, "I didn't mean to startle you."

"I didn't think you'd have any part of me," I said, turning my gaze back to the distant stars and leaving her standing there alone. Two could play at this game. Pa claimed that he and Ma had a running argument as to whether or not it was Adam or Eve who started it all, but as I'd grown older I got to wondering if both of them hadn't had a hand in it somehow.

"Papa says I owe you an apology." My back was to her and I couldn't see her face, but her voice didn't sound any too humble from the tone of it. I said nothing, still keeping to myself.

For a long minute there was silence, then she stepped up beside me. "I used to do a lot of dreaming too." Her voice was softer now, back to normal, and from the corner of my eye I thought I could see her staring off in the same direction as I was. Suddenly, I felt an odd feeling, as though her being there changed everything between us. And maybe it did. All I knew was I'd never felt that way about or with a woman in my entire life. Maybe that's what being in love was like. I didn't know, for I'd never been in love before. But there was something about that feeling that made me uneasy. Still, I was drawn to the woman beside me.

"Why did you stop?" I gave a slow, easy glance to my left as I said it, although I'll be the first to admit that the expression on my own face wasn't as stoic as I'd intended.

A fleeting smile crossed her lips, more sad than happy, I thought. "The grim realities of life were impressed upon me," she said. "Dreamers never get anywhere in this world. One must work hard and—" Her sentence trailed off and she sniffed, and I had a notion she was going to start crying again.

To hell with this game-playing!

"You know, Rebecca," I said, facing her now, "if you put as much gumption into fighting whatever it is that's eating away at you as you did in being uppity at supper tonight, well, you might surprise yourself." It wasn't what I had meant to say, it just came out that way. Hell, I wasn't even sure of what it was I had wanted to say. But she looked at me, cocking her head just a mite to the side, the way a person does who's studying you from close up and doesn't care whether or not you know it. Then a smile came to her lips, the one I'd grown so fond of seeing all through that long trip across the plains to Denver. She had me wondering what she was about to do, but by then it was too late, for she was already doing it. A kiss, a quick one at that, but a kiss just the same.

"Was that your apology?" I didn't know what else to say.

"No." She smiled. "This is." Then she took her hands, placed one on each side of my face, and had to help bring it only halfway down to meet hers as we kissed again. Longer this time, but just as enjoyable as the first had been. It wasn't until we parted that I realized that I had my arms around her and that hers were around me as well.

"Miss Becky, you sure do know how to give an apology!'' Have you ever felt surprised and happy all at once, the way a kid does when he gets a birthday present? Well, friend, that's exactly how I was feeling! I hadn't expected those kisses at all, but they sure were a pleasure to receive. I was just thankful for the dark because my face must've been beet-red.

"I don't often do that," she said, sounding about as awkward as I felt. "I don't usually get carried away like that." After a short silence, she added, "In fact, I've never done that before. I don't know why, I just—"

A lantern shone on the back porch and Samuel Botkin appeared to one side of it, squinting. "I see you youngsters are back on speaking terms," he said. "She apologize to you, Jedediah? I told her to."

"Oh . . . yes, sir, she did," I answered him, then, giving Becky a smile, I said, in a much lower voice, "she surely did."

"Well, don't be long, I'm turning in," he said as the lantern disappeared from sight.

The conversation sort of dried up then as each of us tried to think of something to say, but simply stood there in silence instead.

"Seems to me I heard that them fellas did a lot of stargazing, way back when," I said finally, hoping I made sense. "Daydreaming, if you will."

"Who ever are you talking about?" she asked. I would've felt like a damn fool if it weren't for the fact that she was looking happy again and seeing her that way made me feel good.

"Well, I mean them fellas that made up all the rules," I told her. "Like the one I heard about a while ago. Pluto I think his name was."

That brought a genuine laugh from her, but I can't say as I felt all that badly, for even if she was laughing at me . . . well, I still liked what I saw on her pretty face.

"No, no," she said, taking my hand in hers, still smiling. "You mean *Plato*. Pluto is the name of a planet up in the sky." She paused for a moment, still holding my hand in a firm grasp. Then, in a more serious tone, she said, "But I guess you're right. They were all stargazers back then." She sighed. "It's too bad that things have changed so much."

"Not really," I said. "The stars are still out. Plenty of folks still keep looking at 'em, hoping they'll find one to hang their dreams on. If you think about it, having a dream is how most people from back east got out here in the first place. That one little dream, one small star out there, is all that kept a lot of 'em going." I smiled, slowly pulling her closer to me until I was looking down into her eyes. "No reason you shouldn't dream like the rest of us, no matter how hard you think life is. It might even get you through the tough parts once in a while."

"Yes, I know what you mean," she said, but little more, for I was kissing her then, and just like the last time we were holding each other tight.

And you know something, hoss? Other than that eerie feeling I had just being with her, well, I was starting to feel real comfortable around Becky. Especially when I held her in my arms . . .

Chapter 4

I don't know who was more shy the next morning, Becky or me. What made it worse during breakfast was that Samuel Botkin would take a gander at one or the other of us every once in a while and chuckle as though he knew everything that was going on.

"How did you get your name?" Becky asked when her father had left to open his general store. She poured the last of the coffee as she gave me a curious look.

I shrugged. "Pa always said Ma pulled the name out of the Bible; that it had something to do with that Solomon fella. But he's also told me for some time now that he named me after Jedediah Strong Smith, a mountain man he knew about forty years ago."

"What does your mother think of that?" she asked, just as innocent as could be as she began clearing the table. When I didn't answer, she repeated the question.

"I don't know," I said, only this time I was the one feeling the pain. "I never knew her. She died giving birth to me."

Whatever it was she had in her hand dropped and a horrified look crossed her face as she saw the pain in mine.

"I'm so sorry . . . I—"

"I've gotta git," I said, not wanting to go through what I'd run through in my own mind a thousand times already. I sloshed on my hat and grabbed up the Spencer. "Got a lot to do."

"Jedediah," she said when I was almost out of the room. I stopped, glancing over my shoulder at her. "It means 'beloved of the Lord.' Your name." A weak smile accompanied her words, but they made little difference in the way I felt.

"Yeah," I said. Then I left.

I still didn't know what was eating away at her, but Rebecca Botkin had gotten a good look at what my own weakness was. Not that I minded being raised by an older brother and a father, you understand, but not having a mother, not to mention finding out that I was responsible for her death . . . well, it makes you suspicious about the rest of the world. First you wonder if they all know about the guilt you feel, and then you wonder how they'll use it to play the odds against you. It's not a pretty thing to have to live with, I can tell you that. Fact is, when I had to explain it, as I just had to Becky, I got good and mad and God help the man who got in my way.

Leach got in my way.

I was headed down the boardwalk when he and a cohort stepped out in front of me. I didn't recognize his partner, but when the man made a move toward me, I just brought my boot heel down hard on his instep and rammed a shoulder into him, knocking him off the boardwalk and into the dusty street. Leach was the type who gets some perverted pleasure out of seeing others pushed around, and I don't mind telling you that it had worn real thin on me a long time back. Like I said, Leach got in my way.

"You're just begging to get the hell blowed outta you, ain't you?" I said, swinging the barrel of my Spencer around so it stuck just above the big man's belt buckle. If he didn't know from the look on my face that I'd kill him then and there, well, he was a damn fool. "Tut, tut, friend," I said to the man I'd flattened as he got to his feet and readied to charge. "You come at me and you'll lose your amigo here," I added, cocking the rifle and pulling my bowie with my left hand. "And then *you'll* get carved up something fierce."

"Put it away, Diah."

I looked up and saw Glen Forbush walking across the street, then glanced at Leach, who was now sweating just a mite above his brow, and back at the yahoo in the street.

"Now, Diah," Forbush repeated, and I knew he meant it. "There are more important things to be taken care of at the moment than some petty squabble between you two."

I let the hammer down on the rifle and sheathed my knife.

Glen Forbush wasn't exactly big, his build more on the thin side than anything, but he was a force to be reckoned with in this town. If you could picture a lawman dressed like a gambler, with a vest and black frock coat and all, then you've just described the current marshal in Denver. Forbush made more money at gambling than he ever would at enforcing the law, but he had a reputation of being good with the short-barreled Sheriff's Model Dragoon he carried, so folks listened when he talked. Right now the audience was getting bigger and bigger.

"Jesse, here, says the supply train he was with is under attack out there about the same place you two got hit by the Arapahoes two days back," Forbush said, addressing both Leach and me. The frail man beside him was twice my age and looked like he'd blow away in a good windstorm. "I've got some men who are willing to give those people a hand, but I want you two to take 'em out there. Hell, you're the best Indian fighters we've got right now, and you know the trail better than most." When he saw

Leach and me give each other threatening looks, it made him only that more determined. "Look, you two want to tear each other's guts out, that's fine with me," he said, spitting the words out, cold and hard. "But right now you're both going out to save a few other hides."

"What if I say I ain't going?" the big man challenged.

Forbush slowly pulled out his pistol, balanced it in his hand, and looked it over as though making sure it was in perfect working condition before his gaze fell back on Leach and his friend.

"Well now, Leach, I reckon you can say anything you like. Now, I don't really care what Dusty here does." A bit of a smile came to Forbush's face as he looked at the man I'd knocked into the street. "But I say you go, Leach," he added, cocking his pistol, "and that's that." It was an order he knew the big man wouldn't go against. "You've got half an hour to get your gear and your mounts," he said when Leach was silent.

I started back toward the store, where I had my gear, but had taken only a few steps, when I heard Forbush talking again.

"One other thing, Leach," the marshal said, pistol still in hand. "If young Hooker don't make it back in one piece, you'd better have one helluva good story about why he didn't."

"And what the hell's *that* supposed to mean?" Leach was angry now.

"It means that my having to explain to Old Man Hooker how his son died is likely gonna be the death of me," the lawman replied with a grin.

"And what if *I* don't make it back?"

"I'll pay for a headstone for you." The smile was gone, the hardness back in the marshal's voice. "Now, get moving!"

* * *

I was packing my gear in the extra room not ten minutes later when I heard Becky enter the room. Or maybe I sensed her more than heard her, for she did it very quietly.

"I thought you were a guide," she said. Over my shoulder I saw a look of disappointment, a look of betrayal on her face.

"When it's called for, yeah."

"The men on the streets are now saying that you're a great *Indian fighter*." Glen Forbush would've had to go some to spit out those words as angrily as Becky had just done. To her the term was one to be loathed, I reckon.

"When the situation calls for it, yeah." I shoved the last of my gear into my possibles bag, and when I looked back, she was still standing there, a look of seething anger still on her face. And I'll tell you, friend, woman or not, I never did like being badgered. I set the bag down and in two big steps across the room I was standing before her. This hadn't been my day so far, so why should it be any different now?

"Look, lady, I didn't start that war out there! And I damn well didn't stand around asking just who you were or what you did for a living when those redskins was about to lift your hair on the way here! I can shoot and I can fight, and if that don't suit you to a T, well, lady, you've got a helluva nerve, that's all I can say!"

She slapped me hard with the full flat of her hand, and at first I thought she was going to start clawing at me as well. But then the anger left her eyes and a kind of fear took its place as she realized what she had done.

"Diah, I—"

"Get outta my way," I growled, pushing past her.

For once in my life I'd thought I had someone I could believe in, someone I could trust. Walking out that store, I knew it was all gone now. . . .

Chapter 5

It wasn't the first time I'd had to saddle and ride in a hurry. Indian attacks were getting to be a way of life out here the past couple of years, and anytime from early spring to late fall you could count on the Arapahoe and Ute and Cheyenne going on the warpath in the Denver area. If there hadn't been a war going on back east, it might have been a different story, but as it was we pretty much had to count on our own selves to pull through it alive. The fact that Leach and I were riding out together not an hour after we'd come to near blows . . . well, that showed how serious the situation was.

"Never thought I'd see it," one of the volunteers commented when Leach and I formed up at the head of the group. But he didn't say a hell of a lot more after he got the colder-than-hell looks the two of us gave him in response.

Jesse, the man who had given the alarm about the attack on the wagon train, pulled up beside us and made ready to show us the way, although I seriously doubted that we'd need him what with all the shaking he was doing. Scared or feverish, I didn't know which, he'd had more than a drink or two to settle him down.

"Don't look like he'll be much use to us," I said to Leach, and for once got an agreeable answer from the man I'd grown to hate so much of late.

"Yeah. Whiskeyed up like that, he'd likely give us away if the wind is right. Why don't you go find you a doctor," he said to Jesse, adding in a lower voice, "or another bottle." The relief that shone in the man's eyes was a pure indication of the gratitude he felt for not having to go back to that supply train.

As we started for the location of the Indian attack, Jesse's expression stuck in my mind, and I found myself wondering if we might not be riding out into some kind of ambush. Hell, it wouldn't be the first time that someone had been lured into a trap on the pretense of a rescue mission. I told Leach what I was thinking and he agreed to keep on the lookout for anything out of the ordinary. One thing I could say about the man was that when it came to doing his job, he was downright thorough about it, setting aside all personality conflicts.

As it turned out, all my worrying was for nothing. At least at the start.

Seven wagons doesn't give you all that much room when you circle them, but these fellows had made due pretty well for the time they'd been under siege. They were all freight wagons, and the supplies were covered and tied down by canvas and rope. From a distance I could see what looked like gunfire coming from eight or nine different weapons, but that didn't tell me a hell of a lot about the number of men inside the circle. An eighth wagon, its team now gone, was some twenty yards outside the circle of wagons, a handful of warriors using it for cover as they tried to potshot the drivers.

The trouble was that those fellows on the inside had about had it. The Arapahoe war party, numbering about the same as our own group, had been beating down on

those men for more than a day now and were moving in
for the final kill, from the looks of it. Every man's eye
was trained on the braves as they rode in closer with less
opposition. We had just topped the rise and taken all this
in with a glance, each man in our party drawing out a pistol
or checking the loads in his long gun as we did so. But it
was the bloodthirsty look in Leach's eye that set it all off.

"Kill the sonsabitches!!" he screamed at the top of his
lungs, and he was the first man down the slope toward what
now looked like a hopeless situation as the warriors who
had gotten close enough began to make their way inside
the circle of wagons. No more gunfire was directed toward
anyone outside the circle now, all the fighting being done
within.

Those braves were goners was the only thought that
flashed through my mind as I followed Leach down the
slope. Leach had a pistol in one hand and his reins in the
other as he spurred his mount into a full run and jumped
into the the center of the foray, where the handful of
freighters were fighting hand to hand with their attackers.
Leach lost his hat as he entered the circle, but by the time
he was in it, a second pistol was in his hand and he was
shooting left and right like the madman I thought him to
be.

Three of us surprised those braves hiding behind the outer
wagon, killing three of the five instantly. One of our own
men took a shot in the gut while I downed the fifth Indian
as he tried to escape. Several of the other volunteers had
joined the fight inside the circle, and as I quickly dismounted, most of the attackers seemed to be on the run.

The canvas was still intact on the wagon we had killed
the Indians behind, and I was curious now to why no one
had removed the contents. The tailgate was down, and
when I got to it, I saw all too readily why no one had
bothered with it further.

The wagon was full of gunpowder! If the two short kegs I saw at the end near the tailgate were any indication of what the rest of the cargo was, this wagon was one big explosive ready to go off!

"Charley, we gotta get outta here!" I said to a nearby rider who'd ridden in with me. I didn't know who he was or whether that was his name or not, but it seemed to fit at the moment.

"Not hardly, friend," was his reply as he looked toward that slope we'd just come over. "I got a feeling we've been had. Let's get Hank around back of this wagon."

"What the—" Then I saw them and knew he was right. I grabbed that possibles bag and the sack of tubes I carried with my Spencer refills and let my horse go before giving Charley a hand with the wounded man. We propped him up against the wagon wheel on my side, Charley breaking the arrow off while the man assured him weakly that he was all right and I took another gander to make sure my eyes weren't playing tricks on me.

Them was another war party of Arapahoe; thirty, forty, fifty—hell, I don't know—coming down over that same slope as we had, pulling the same kind of surprise attack we had done!

"Can you reload these?" I asked the wounded man, handing him an empty tube. When he nodded, I added, "Refills are in that possibles bag next to you."

"Sure thing." he grimaced.

"Goddamn it!" To my rear I saw Leach standing out in front of the wagon behind us, two empty pistols in his hands, a look of pure frustration on his face as he took in the charging war party. He ran halfway out toward us, where he had no cover at all, yelling, "Get in here, you goddamn fools! Indian attack!" before he was hit high in the shoulder with an arrow. Like I said, Leach was a big man, so seeing him standing there dumbfounded, looking

at that arrow as if it were some sort of pesky fly, well, it
was almost comical. What seemed idiotic was him just
standing there in the open like that. Like it or not, I knew
we were going to need every good shot we could round
up, including Leach.

"Git over here, Leach!" I yelled to him, finally getting
his attention as he caught sight of my arms acting like a
windmill. To tell the truth, I wasn't sure but that we'd have
room for Leach or not. Hell, there was already me and
Charley and Hank behind that freight wagon, and as big
as Leach was, why, he might just squeeze one of us out
on the sides. By the time he got there I knew I was right.

He tried desperately to lean into the wagon for cover as
he picked up a discarded revolver, but in the process he
pushed the arrow only that much farther into him. He
grunted, and I thought I saw him go pale in the face for a
second, but the man still functioned as though he hadn't
been hit.

"Gimme a pistol," he demanded.

"Here," I said, setting the Spencer down while I pulled
out a Colt I carried and handed it to him. His concentration
was on the pistol's loads, so I used the time to place the
flat of one hand against his shoulder while I busted the
arrow off and Leach went pale in the face again. The pain
was finally getting to him, and he wouldn't be on his feet
much longer, of that I was sure.

"See if you can reload for us," I said when he dropped
to one knee, looking about ready to pass out. He was fighting it, but I didn't think he could outlast the pain.

"Why?" he said in that demanding voice again, "I
can—"

An arrow thudded into the back of the wagon between
the two of us as a warrior rode past us to the rear. I grabbed
up that Spencer, stepped back from the wagon, and shot

him out of the saddle, hoping there wasn't another one like him coming at my own back.

"That's why!" I yelled back at Leach. "Damn, but you can make a body mad!" I gave him a quick, hard stare, recocking my rifle as I did. "See if you can't watch our backs and do some reloading at the same time, Leach. Believe, me," I assured him, "ain't nobody gonna think less of you for it."

They'd made their first pass at us by then and were re-grouping for a second run. A fast survey of the area showed that most of our group had found cover at one place or another, most of them inside the circle of wagons.

"Can't you reload any faster than that?" Charley said in as frustrated a tone of voice as I'd heard Leach speaking in earlier.

"Not hardly," the big man said, now sitting with his back to the wagon. When I glanced at him, wondering why he always persisted in being so stubborn, I saw what he meant.

Hank was dead, his face having fallen forward, chin on his chest, the only thing keeping him from falling all the way to the side being Leach.

"Do the best you can," I said, hearing the war whoops start up again. "We're gonna need it."

They came over that slope again, but this time we were ready for them, and I mean we were *ready* for them. Leach did one hell of a job watching our backs, and more than one Indian pony passed to our rear riderless. What scared the hell out of me was a bullet that chipped away a piece of wood from the top of that freight wagon. As far as any of us knew, most of the war parties had few repeaters, pistols, or rifles, and had stuck pretty much to the bows and arrows they were accustomed to. But that one bullet made me take particular notice of those of the attackers who had carbines, rifles, or pistols, and I made them my primary targets from then on. Hell, I didn't want to get blown to kingdom come without leaving some sort of a body to bury. Would you?

We thinned them out some on that second go-around, me using up at least half of those ammunition tubes I carried. When I glanced his way, I noticed that Leach was still reloading pistols, but had yet to touch any of my magazine tubes. All he did was give me as evil a smile as I'd ever seen, the kind that told you he was going to do you in, one way or another.

"Wearing you down, are they?" he said, seeing the look of concern on my face. Either the pain had eased up in his shoulder or he was beyond caring about it anymore, for he seemed as mischievous as ever.

"Only one trying to wear me down has been you, Leach, and I don't mind telling you I'm goddamn tired of it." But my words didn't faze him in the least; he was going to get rid of me in one fashion or another. Old Leach; I reckon what he needed was some motivation. But my mind was racing so fast trying to figure out what these red devils were going to do next, I couldn't think of a way to give it to him.

On that third run they must've figured they were going to do us in once and for all. They not only had a frontal attack launched at us, but were hitting us from the sides and probably the rear as well, although I couldn't tell. I had my first inkling that they might just succeed, too, when I felt the pain of an arrow as it near knocked me off my feet, striking the back of my calf.

"Missed, damn it," was all I heard Leach say, although he wasn't smiling anymore.

"Sonofabitch," I muttered, regaining my balance enough to step back and kill the bastard who'd tried doing the same thing to me as he rode by.

Another bullet chipped away at the top of that freight

wagon at the same time Leach reached over, grabbed hold of my leg with one hand, and jerked on the arrow as hard as he could with the other. And sure enough, he had that mad little smile on his face when I recovered enough to throw an angry glance his way.

That tore it! I was tired of this big lug having his own way all the time. You see, that was when it hit me, how I was going to make Leach do a bit of sweating of his own. Wear me down? Not in a lifetime!

"Charley, you see any of them fellas looks like he's got himself a pistol, rifle, anything that ain't a bow and arrow, I'd advise you to do your best to send 'em to that happy hunting ground."

"Why?" my fellow rifleman asked, looking a bit confused.

"You know why they left this wagon out here?" I didn't wait for an answer. "It wasn't the Arapahoe that took it, it was those freighters set it out here!"

"Why the hell'd they do that?" Charley asked, still confused.

"Cause this wagon's loaded with kegs of gunpowder," I told him with a smile, looking straight at Leach as I said it.

The Indians were regrouping now, so Charley ran around to my side of the wagon, his eyeballs about ready to fall out once he glimpsed the kegs of gunpowder.

"I'll be damned," he said with a slow sort of awe, if there is such a thing. But that was all Leach needed to hear before breaking out in a cold sweat and digging into that possibles bag of mine for cartridges to reload my magazines. Giving a man a fright can humble him if it's done right, is how Pa used to tell it. And it looked like I'd done it right, for Leach was all of a sudden real motivated.

"Ain't wearing you down, pard, are they?" I asked,

only this time I was the one smiling and him the one looking uncomfortable.

We'd thinned them out a bit more on that last run, and to tell the truth, I wasn't sure if either of us were feeling all that confident about our fourth encounter. I didn't know about Charley and Leach, but I wasn't certain how much ammunition or fire power or men we had left in that circle of wagons we were near. You get in a fight like this and most all of the gunfire you hear is your own. It's louder than everybody else's, excepting maybe that of the fellows shooting back at you who manage to get close enough, and that can be a fearsome thing.

The Arapahoes were gearing up for the same kind of run, a three-sided attack, as they made their presence known on the horizon and gave off those godawful war whoops again.

"Jesus, Mary and—" I heard Leach yell before turning to my rear.

"You don't think they're—"

"Leaving us! The bastards are leaving us!" His voice was near panic and I couldn't say that I blamed him. What he'd spotted was as many horses and men getting out of that circle as fast as could be, maybe even all of them, not a one of them staying around to see the fireworks heading down the slope at us! I was cussing as bad as Leach, grabbing hold of his one good arm and lifting him to his feet as he tossed the loaded pistols on top of the canvas, while every one of the riders disappeared around to the rear of those circled wagons, likely heading in the opposite direction.

"Didn't think they disliked me that much," Leach said, waiting for the charging warriors to get within pistol range. He had all of four pistols to use, but God only knew if we'd ever make it out of this scrape.

"Me neither."

I was getting ready to meet my Maker then. Pa always said to fight like hell and let them know who it was they tangled with before they paraded your scalp into some wikiup, and that's exactly what I was bent on doing.

Except it didn't happen that way.

All three of us were back to back at that point, Charley and I shooting as fast and hard as we could at two sides and Leach laying into those Indian ponies coming his direction, causing more confusion than you'd have thought possible once the riders behind them started falling all over those already down.

I was replacing a magazine when all of those volunteers we'd come with and just seen desert us came riding hellfor-leather around the side of those wagons, only this time they were charging upslope instead of down. By God, maybe we'd make it yet!

About a third of the group split up and lit out in each direction we were being attacked from, cutting down the odds considerably. As much gunpowder as there was in the air now, it looked like hell took a holiday while those Indians who hadn't decided to stand and take their chances were riding off to healthier climates.

The biggest problem we had then turned out to be a halfdozen young braves who'd had their horses shot out from under them and were still in a fighting mood, for they were charging straight toward us now on foot. That was when Charley got wounded.

Leach surprised those six running toward us by throwing lead at them from my Colts and a battered old Remington that still worked, killing or at least wounding four of them. If you want to see bravery, you should have seen Leach standing there as big as life, a target for any and all who'd want him dead, just shooting like there wasn't no tomorrow. Me, I was covering the outsides of this group of hostiles, trying to add to the riderless horses that were growing in number. But one of those braves on foot made it through, jumping on Charley when his rifle misfired. That young buck hacked a slice into Charley's arm but never made it any farther. Leach back-shot him as he was about to take a swipe at Charley's neck.

I reckon that Indian had served as a diversion, for it was then that the sixth brave appeared from the front of the wagon directly to my left. He must've been hiding, waiting for the right moment to make his move and figured this was it. He lunged at me and likely would have killed me had his knife not caught itself in the side of the big buck-skin jacket I wore. As it was, he only tore the pocket some. By the time he'd recovered his balance, so had I. I'd also swung my Spencer around, and pulled the trigger. The force of the .52-caliber bullet and charge was a heavy one that lifted him up a mite and carried him backwards a couple of feet before he fell to the already bloodstained ground, dead.

Then I reloaded another magazine, noticing that the firing was becoming distant, the fighting apparently dying down.

"Had me going there for a while," Leach sighed with the same amount of relief the rest of us felt.

"Me too," Charley said, putting down his rifle and untying his bandanna to stop the bleeding in his arm.

"And you're still ugly as sin and dislikable," I added, feeling good that it was all over now, but, seeing Leach, knowing that it wasn't really all over. Not yet. The sight of his bloody shoulder reminded me of the arrow stuck in the calf of my own leg and I knew it wouldn't be long before the blood rushing out of me would be slowing me down. I also knew the same thing would be happening to every other wounded man among us, including Leach.

"Leach." I smiled at him.

"Yeah?" He seemed confused, for by then I'd tossed

my rifle on top of the canvas tarpaulin. By the time he saw it he knew what I had in mind but could do nothing about it. Not one damn thing.

I hit him hard with my right and left, knocking his big ugly face back and forth twice before it crossed my mind that I'd either busted my knuckles or totally lost all of my strength. He stood there, that same surprised look about him, and began to raise a fist. Then his eyes sort of glazed over and he fell forward, shaking the ground as he did so.

"See," I smiled to Charley, "he ain't so tough."

The next thing I saw was Leach's body coming up to meet mine as I passed out. . . .

Chapter 6

They took their own sweet time getting us back to Denver. At least that's what it seemed like to me. Fact is, the only thing I was sure of was that they'd laid me out on top of one of those wagons for the trip and that we'd spent at least one night under the stars.

"Here, I'll give you a hand," Samuel Botkin said, taking me by the shoulder and easing me off the side of the freight wagon as Charley held on to my other arm. His buckskins were bloodied, but he appeared to be no worse for wear than when I'd last seen him standing back at the wagon train circle.

"Keep him away from your women, Mister Botkin," Charley said in his gruff voice. "He's been cussing something fierce the past twenty-four hours." He rumbled what must have been a laugh and eyed Samuel. "Don't think I ever seen a body so scared to death when he come to."

"Me? Scared? Who are you joshing, Charley?" I said as we entered my room in the back of Samuel's store. After all, man's got his pride.

"Ain't joshing nobody, son." The look on Charley's face had changed to the kind that said he was as ready to be as dead serious as he was to bust out laughing. To

Samuel he said, "Kid comes to on that canvas after we taken the arrow out of him and asks where he is." I didn't remember a damn thing Charley was saying, so for all I knew, he was stretching the blanket. A smile curled his lip up as he glanced from me to Botkin. "I tell him he's laying right on top of those kegs of gunpowder he'd been fighting behind, and all of a sudden he turns sheet-white and tells me I gotta get him the hell off'n 'em."

"I don't understand," Samuel said, although I think he suspected it was some kind of joke.

"Why, he said his leg was on fire, and it was so hot it would heat up that gunpowder so's we'd all get blowed to kingdom come!" Charley laughed again when he said it, but it was the sound I heard beyond him, and the brief sight of Becky peeking around the corner and disappearing again, that caught my attention.

"How'd Leach make out?" I asked.

"Same as you, 'cepting he kept *asking* was he laid out on top of them powder kegs." Another chuckle. "Knew he'd bellyache once he come to, so the first time he asked I told him, yes, sir, that's exactly where he was." A shake of the head, another chuckle. "Passed out and slept like a baby the whole night through, I hear.

"Both of 'em lost a lot of blood," Charley said to Samuel now in a serious tone. "Git this 'un some doctoring and a few days' worth of rest and he'll be good as new." He disappeared out the door and was soon back, propping my Spencer up against the wall, setting the possibles bag and magazines next to it. "Don't forget this," he said to me. Again he turned to leave, momentarily stopping in the doorway. "What horses they could round up are back of the livery, I'm told. Might check there for yours when you get to moving around."

Then Charley was gone.

"I'll get my medicinals and see if we can't give that

wound some proper treatment," Samuel said and then he, too, left the room.

Then I got attacked!

I was sitting on the edge of my bed, wondering how painful it would be to reach over and grab up that possibles bag to see how much I was missing, when all of a sudden I looked up and this big blur came rushing at me! At first I thought it was another Indian, or Leach, bent on getting final revenge. But it wasn't.

It was Becky, and she came around that corner so fast she bowled me over back onto the bed, then commenced kissing me. We parted once and she muttered, "You damn fool," but then she was kissing me again, and light-headed or not, I'd temporarily forgotten about the pain in my leg.

"Aren't there better places for that?" a voice said to our rear. It was Samuel Botkin all right, looking as stern as a father well might when discovering his daughter where she was. I can tell you right now that if I didn't have any blood flowing out of my leg where they'd pulled out the arrow then, well, it was because it was all in my face! And Becky, well, I do believe I even saw her complexion deepen some. "Well, if you're that fond of him, here, you patch him up," Samuel said, handing an assortment of bottles and bandages to his daughter, who was still speechless. The look on his face may have been a stern one, but the twinkle in his eye told me he was having his own kind of father-daughter fun.

"Take your pants off," she said to me with as straight a face as I'd ever seen.

"Ma'am?" I said, throwing a cautious glance at her, wondering if she was going out of her way to get me killed.

"I can't clean and bandage your wound properly unless they're off." Still the straight face, but now her tough-as-nails attitude was back, that same one I'd confronted before leaving with the volunteers. And somehow I knew that nothing had been resolved in the few days we'd been apart, that her spur-of-the-moment kisses had been nothing more than that. Somewhere inside this girl-woman there was a grudge she was carrying and she'd chosen me to take it out on.

Well, friend, I wasn't having any of it!

I was sitting upright now, taking in that beautiful face and wondering what it was that made her insides so different from what I saw. At the same time, I was pulling out my bowie knife.

"What are you doing?" She was bossy as hell now, sounding more like one of those frustrated generals in the War Between the States than the woman I'd spoken to the night before I left.

"Levi ain't much good no more," I said, looking down at the bloodied denim that had been torn by the arrow, both going in and being pulled out. Part of a torn shirt had been folded up and placed over the wound, secured in place by someone's bandanna. I bent down slowly, praying I wouldn't lose consciousness, for I was feeling weak, found the edge of that bandanna and the torn pants leg and gently ran the tip of my knife up the back of the calf. The material split open easily. I then ran the edge of the knife along the denim just below my knee, cutting away enough all around so it fell away from my calf. "That'll give you room to work in."

She said nothing for a moment, knowing that I could be just as stubborn as she. Then she instructed me to lie on my belly so she could give proper attention to the wound.

"I thought you didn't have any great love for *Indian fighters*," I said over my shoulder after I'd worked my way into a facedown position on the bed. Hell, I could match her for acting crusty any day of the week. It was the wrong thing to say.

She was silent as she undid the bandanna, slowly removing it from the dried blood it covered, but the whole time she was doing it I could feel the cold, hard glare she was giving me. That's when she did it. Tossing the bandanna to the side, she took a fistful of denim in one hand and yanked back on it. Dried blood and mucus and whatever the hell else had been thrown on that wound while I was passed out came undone, causing a fearsome pain to shoot up my leg and back. But it didn't stop me from letting out one hell of colorful piece of wordage.

"What the hell did you do that for!" I yelled out, starting to turn over, ready to take a poke at her, woman or not. To my surprise, I never made it, as she pushed me facedown with her free hand without much effort at all. The crusted piece of denim fell back on the open wound, sending pain shooting up my leg again.

Pa always said it was the mad in a body that got them to doing what they had in mind. I'd wondered about that at times, not sure if it was just one person's opinion or if there really was all that much to it. My brother Guns and I, well, it didn't make any difference how old we were, we knew real early in life that you don't doubt Pa or try to fight him. No, sir, especially when you've learned that lesson the hard way, and I don't mind telling you that both my brother and I had learned it just that way. But right now I had the notion that Pa knew just what he was talking about, for Becky had gone from pushing me facedown with the flat of her hand to leaning into the small of my back with her elbow and forearm, and I couldn't move one bit. Either she was madder than hell or I was as weak as Charley had said.

"You don't know much about pain or hurt, *Mister* Hooker, do you?" she breathed into my ear with a hiss. The words were all coming out right and proper, as though they were being spoken by a schoolteacher, but I didn't like the hardness in them. It was too close to hate for me, especially considering what I'd thought I felt for the woman.

"What in the deuce is going on in here!" Samuel said, appearing in the doorway. A frown at his daughter got her off my back real quick. "I've got customers out there," he added, the distress in his voice saying that he was about to lose them. "I thought you were fixing him up, not taking his scalp!"

He was gone then, back to his business, and I almost smiled at what he had said, catching myself just in time. Becky had an outraged look about her and I knew that if she saw me finding humor in her father's statement, well, maybe she would take a scalp. And I wasn't at all interested in finding out.

Silently, she went back to tending to my wound and I thought that was the end of it. It wasn't. A minute or two later she poured liniment on the wound and once again I let out a yell.

"Goddammit!" I rolled onto my left side, reached down with my hand, and hit the side of my calf, as though doing so would jar the liniment out of the open crevice, realizing after I'd done it that it made the leg hurt only that much more. It also produced a look of shock in Becky's face. Or maybe it was seeing the bowie in my hand again that put the fear in her eyes.

"I don't know what's eatin' at you, *lady*," I said, hard and mean as could be, "but I've about had my fill of it! You get some kind of joy outta inflicting pain on me, do you? Well, you do it one more time, just one more time—" I was going to read to her from the book, tell her how far she'd pushed me and how tired of it all I was, but I never finished. Not then, anyway.

"Put it away!" Samuel said. His voice was filled with authority now, the same kind I'd heard when he'd had his run-in with Leach. His tone was all business, but this was a different kind of business. "I don't ever want to see that out of its sheath unless supper's being served." He'd made his point, but I wasn't any too happy about it.

"Why don't you just charge 'em admission and let 'em come back and see how real Indian torture is performed?" It was sarcastic as hell, and maybe he didn't think it was called for, but you can bet the farm I wasn't about to apologize for it, not on your life! But it was Becky who had his attention now.

"Rebecca," he said in that long, drawn-out fashion parents have of addressing their children before they give them a talking-to.

I'd heard it plenty from Pa in my time and I reckon Becky had, too, for it brought a humble "Yes, Papa" from her lips, along with what looked like a pout.

"The next time I have to come back here, I'll take you over my knee. You're still not too big for it, you know."

She knew he meant it, and muttered "Yes, Papa," again under her breath, then made an attempt at sticking out that lower lip further, as though to make her pout that much more noticeable.

"And you," he growled, addressing me with a frown, "you give out a holler like that again and I'll have you chopping wood until next spring before you get your precious rifle back!" With that he stepped inside the room, grabbed up my Spencer, and was about to retreat, when he stopped and cast a daring eye down at me. "If you're so damn tough, you wouldn't be screaming like that. Smith wouldn't have done that. Stick that bowie between your teeth and see if you can't make an impression on it while she's fixing you up."

I sheathed the knife and he left. We were back to silence again and I found myself wondering when she'd do it again, but she didn't. I could feel her softly ridding the wounded area of crusted matter, and I flinched once but decided I could bear it if it didn't get much worse.

"I didn't do that on purpose," she finally said, her tone of voice considerably softer than before.

"Yeah."

"It was a mistake. You must believe that."

"Yeah."

Silence, more cleaning up, more flinching.

"You're all alike," she said, "you don't understand." She was giving sounding hard-bitten another try.

Like I said, I wasn't having any of it. I glanced over my shoulder, cocking a curious eye at her. "Ain't nobody ever understood nobody less'n they were given a chance." I went back to staring at the wall before me.

"Who is Smith? What did Papa mean about Smith?" Conversational is what she was trying to be. Maybe it *had* been a mistake, that liniment winding up on me like that. Maybe.

"Jed Smith," I said, still facing forward. "Jedediah Strong Smith, the fella I got named after."

"Oh."

"Got himself into a fight with a grizzly bear back in 'twenty-three or 'twenty-four, Pa says. He never was sure of the year. Bear busted some ribs, near tore off the left side of his scalp, and *did* tear off his left ear."

"It must have been very painful," she said, wincing at the thought of such an atrocity. I'd done the same thing as a youngster when Pa told me the story, but now I knew it by heart. Lordy, did I know that story. "But I still don't understand," Becky added.

"Well, that's where the story gets sort of gruesome," I said, glancing over my shoulder. "You sure you want to hear it?"

"Yes, I believe I would." My tale had her interest all

right, but I had the eerie notion that it was something other than Jed Smith she was listening for.

"Diah Smith, he was pretty well-bloodied when it was all over. He never was sure whether he killed that bear or not. But it near killed him, that's for sure." I'd visualized it a thousand times before in my mind, and now I found I was curious as to how Rebecca Botkin would see it, what she would see. A person's eyes will tell you a lot. I rolled over on to my left side as she ceased doing her patch-up work and listened to my every word.

"Smith told his men to get some water and fetch a thread and needle. Had a man sew that patch of scalp back on him, and you know something, it stuck! Never did grow any hair back, but it stuck, good as new." She seemed amazed at it, as most folks were.

"That ear of his was hanging down by a thread, I reckon, about to fall off. Smith had 'em sew the ear back on and it took too. Pa was there, seen it. Said it was the bravest thing he ever did see in his entire life." I knew those words all too well, had lived with them since birth, I reckon.

"I should say it was brave!" She echoed, just like everyone else who'd heard the story had. "Fighting a grizzly bear and surviving to tell about it! Yes, that is brave."

"No, ma'am, you don't understand." None of them ever did. "It wasn't fighting that griz that Pa figured was so brave. More than one man's done it and lived to tell about it."

"But, what—"

"The whole time those men were patching Smith up, he just sat there and didn't utter a sound other than to give directions. That's what Pa meant by the bravest thing he'd ever seen."

"I see." She said it in that awed way most folks have

about them when they're not sure whether to take a tale for whole cloth or not.

"And *that* is what your papa meant when he said Smith wouldn't have done the yelling I did," I finished.

"I see." I honest-to-God think she did. "I have to prepare supper soon, so let me finish with this." The formality had come back into her voice.

"You know, Rebecca, most everybody's got some kind of problem in life. Some make their own; some get saddled with 'em before they've anything to say about it."

She squinted, confused. "I don't understand."

"I got saddled with being named after a man who had the reputation for being strong and what they call a born leader to boot. Your pa and mine have known each other for some time, and I can't remember either of 'em not bragging about Jedediah Strong Smith when I'm around. It's as if they and everyone who knows the story is looking for me to live up to another man's reputation just because I've got his name. Do you understand?"

"Yes. Yes, I do." The way she said it was true and honest, almost as if she knew the difficulties I'd faced; and was still facing for that matter.

"Of course, I never went around making other people's lives miserable just because I felt that way about my own." This was directed at her and she knew it, although she wasn't eager to respond to it.

"Grit your teeth, Diah, and we will see if you can be as brave as the other Jedediah. After all, you're not having an ear sewed on." Then she went to work and it hurt like hell!

But I never uttered a sound.

I had two helpings of whatever it was she served up for the evening meal, not being all that picky about it. It wasn't until she had mentioned supper that I'd remembered I hadn't eaten in more than twenty-four hours, another reason my strength was sapped. I could have eaten a horse, but settled for the beef and potatoes Becky served up. And coffee.

I was strong enough to make my way to the table, but the meal was eaten in silence, all three of us trying to bypass a discussion of what had happened that afternoon. To tell the truth, I just wasn't up to any more fighting; maybe that raid and the wound had taken it out of me. Likely it was rest I needed more than anything.

"You youngsters will excuse me if I leave early," Samuel said when he'd finished. "Forbush was in this afternoon and tells me there's a game set for tonight. New blood, as he puts it." He put on his jacket and hat. "Don't wait up for me, Becky." To me he said, "With that leg in the shape it is, I'd advise you to give up stargazing for a night or so."

"New blood?" Becky asked, clearing away the table.

She must've been back east a long time or else she'd led an awful sheltered life, for I had to spend some time telling her about how Pa had gotten the name Black Jack, along with some of the other more common phrases known to gamblers in particular and those who think they can gamble in general. It all seemed to fascinate her, but then, she'd been taking a deep interest in nearly everything since we'd begun the trip out here. It was sort of like she was discovering a whole new life.

I don't recall what exactly we talked about after that except that I did it from a sitting position on the back porch in a chair. Must've been just this and that or I'd have remembered it. What does stick in my mind about that night is that when the sun got to setting and I was making my way back inside, she commented about finding a new pair of Levis for me in her father's store. It was past dusk when she brought them to the room and took a seat beside me.

"Cleanliness is next to godliness," she said, handing me the jeans. "Tomorrow you'll have to bathe. I can help you."

I didn't know what to say. Hell, I'd been doing my own taking care of since way back. The thought of having a woman bathe me, well, it threw me. Or maybe her saying it was supposed to distract me, for when I looked back at her, she was unbuttoning the dress front she wore, pulling the sleeves down over her shoulders. In a few minutes the evening light would be gone. I reckon that was why she was doing it now.

High above each breast in the shoulder region was a scar. It was the ugly kind that is left by a gunshot wound or a thin-bladed knife—or a sharp stake, the kind that pulls your flesh in with it as it is driven into you. She held her head high.

"I have survived what your Smith did, but in a different way. I'm afraid I wasn't as brave as he, but I have suffered the pain. I know how he must have felt."

"Is that why you—"

"I think I understand you better," she said, the softness of her hand touching mine. "I was wrong. I—"

She was humiliating herself now, apologizing for being herself. I kissed her and she was soon holding me as we slowly fell back on the bed. She was warm and forgiving then and as gentle as a woman could be.

Cleanliness might have been next to godliness, but for a short time that night I had Becky next to me . . . and I loved it.

Chapter 7

For two days afterward I stayed pretty much to my room in back of Samuel's store, getting my strength back and cleaning my weapons time and time again. Not that I didn't give that Old Spencer a good going-over the first time, you understand. It's just that Becky kept showing up more than I ever figured a woman could in a living area and, well, it was distracting. Yes, sir, I sure did clean those weapons a lot.

I remembered Pa talking years back about how disgraceful the women were who wore some silly garb they called bloomers. I never did see one of those outfits my own self, but the way Pa described them, half dress without the wire hoops and half pantaloon from Tom Jefferson's plantation, why, they must've been silly. Fact is, that was what I figured Becky had put on the morning after they'd brought me back, when I heard Samuel raise his voice to her.

"You're not thinking of leaving the house in that get-up, are you?" he said in what was more of a challenge than a question.

"No, Papa, of course not," I heard her reply in that soft voice of hers. She had said it smiling, too, I could tell. "I know better than that, Papa. I'm just going to be here helping you today . . . and checking Jedediah's wound,'' she added after a short pause and in a much lower voice.

When I entered the kitchen area in the dim light of early morning, I could see why Samuel Botkin had shown concern over his daughter's dressing habits. It wasn't bloomers Becky was wearing, not at all. It was a pair of brand new denims, and I do believe the top of them would have fallen down were it not for the man's blue workshirt she'd stuffed into the waist, and the doubled-up piece of buckskin that served as a makeshift belt.

That was going to distract me plenty, I knew, for she had no prairie skirt or any of that undergarment rigging women had to wear on. No, sir, that was her standing there, all right—every bit of her!

It didn't show when I walked out there that morning, but I could tell that she was blushing inside when she saw me. Her smile was shy, the same one she'd worn the first day I'd met her back at Fort Riley. I'd since learned that the sudden change in attitude this woman was capable of was enough to keep any man aware of her presence.

''Here, let me give you a hand,'' Samuel said when he spotted me entering the room. And I'm glad he did, for I was having a mite of trouble getting around, and from that room of mine back in the rear to the kitchen area, all of twenty feet down the hallway, seemed like one hell of a long distance. The nerves and muscles in my calf were going to need some healing time, of that I was sure.

''How'd your poker game with Forbush come out last night, Samuel?'' I asked, more as a matter of courtesy than anything else, for I wasn't a card player like my older brother or my father. Besides, I was taking in Becky the whole time I was talking.

''Oh, he let me win some,'' Samuel said, helping me into a chair. It's clumsy having to sit at a table with one leg stuck out nearly straight underneath it. "Fact is, I came away with fifty dollars more than when I started."

"He *lets* you win, Forbush does?" Becky was serving up the food in silence, but brushed just close enough to me when she put my plate in front of me to let me feel the softness of her. Yup, that was her under that shirt all right.

"In a way, you might say that. From what he tells me, he invites just about every stranger who comes into town looking for a game to one of his. You notice how he stays away from fistfights?"

"Yes, sir." I don't think I'd looked at him once since he'd helped me to the table, although I could hear every word he was saying. It's just that . . . well, like I say, Becky was distracting that morning.

"Doesn't want to mess up his hands. Professional gambler at one time, I'd say. Hell, he still is. He interrupted the game only once last night to get rid of some poor excuse for a card shark who'd drifted into town. Why, even I spotted him dealing seconds from the bottom of the deck."

There was a moment of silence then as he stopped talking and Becky and I were aware of only each other.

"Why is it I get the impression I'm talking to myself?" Samuel said, giving the both of us a look that said he was on to what we were up to.

"Oh, no, sir." I smiled politely.

"Of course not, Papa." Becky did the same and went back to busying herself with the food. I still don't remember what it was we had for that meal, for I could scarcely take my eyes off her to look at it.

"Food gets much colder, Diah, and I'm gonna assume you've gone from being the walking wounded to being dead."

"No, sir," I replied promptly, "not at all." I suddenly realized that I was really pretty hungry and took the opportunity to wolf down some food, only to find my gaze back on Becky when I paused for a drink of my coffee.

"You know, for a man who seemed to be in quite a bit of pain walking down that hallway, you sure do smile a lot." If I knew Samuel, he was baiting me, the same as Pa had done when I was a youngster. Trick questions that led to nowhere but embarrassment. Not that I could blame the man, for he had a real woman in Becky. Yes, sir, a real woman.

"Well, it's . . . it's her get-up. Yeah, that's it." I gave both of them a glance and let them see the smile on my face.

"I know, Diah," Samuel moaned, obviously remembering the short conversation he'd had with Becky before I appeared. "Believe me, I *know*."

"You remember how Pa describes a woman?" I asked.

"Sure, but . . ." The sentence trailed off as he searched the back roads of his memory for a meaning. I figured I'd help him out.

"If Pa saw her, he'd likely say she'd never have her a cold in her life, no sir." I smiled at Samuel, and saw the cautious look Becky was now giving us, the kind that told me she wasn't sure what was going on now that a smile had also crossed her father's lips.

"By God, you're right, boy," he said, laughing outright. "I do believe you're right."

"Papa." The caution in her voice was gone now, replaced by a note of fear that I had heard before, only now I had an idea of just where that fear was coming from. Samuel saw it, too, got up, and went to his daughter.

"Rebecca," he said in his most pleasing smile, "no one is going to hurt you here. We were just . . . look, why don't you take a seat and have breakfast too." She did as she was told, a fragile look about her. I didn't know whether she would break down and cry or not.

Samuel had finished most of his food and now dished out some for Becky, refilling our coffee cups before he took his own seat again.

"Black Jack, Jedediah's father, had one woman in his life that he loved, Becky. He felt comfortable only with Martha, I think, and at best he could only joke around other women." He shrugged and gave a hopeless look to his daughter across the table. "He was generally shy around them, and when Martha died, I think he grew even shier." He chuckled, remembering it as funny. Me, I was remembering it with mixed emotions, realizing that he was trying to get something across to Becky but knowing, too, that in the process he was touching a wound inside me that I was never sure would heal.

"Black Jack would see a woman who . . . well, one you could tell was a woman, even in a man's shirt and pants—you know what I mean," he said, looking a bit flushed himself now.

"A woman 'amply endowed'?" Becky said with a raised eyebrow.

"Yeah, that's right," I said. "But Pa, he didn't know those fancy words, you see, and likely never will. He'd see a woman like that and he'd say he bet she hardly ever caught cold." Samuel smiled and so did I, just as before.

"But I still don't understand," Becky said.

"And then, when someone would ask that question, he'd always do his best to keep the lady's best interests in mind. That's when he'd say she was right *healthy*," I told her.

"Well," she said, blushing, "Papa says you have to make due with what you have."

I mumbled something and looked down into that half-empty cup of coffee, hoping Samuel wouldn't see the red creeping up my neck, but I needn't have worried. He finished his coffee and went around the table to stand beside Becky, holding her close to him as he placed a tender hand on her shoulder.

"Actually, I don't mind it all that much, sweetheart." He looked down at her with the kind of loving smile that only a father could give his offspring. "You remind me so much of your mother, and as long as you're safe and happy, that's all that matters to me."

"Oh, I love you so much, Papa," she said, standing up and holding on to him for a while just as she had done me a time or two. Watching them like that, well, I could have sworn that the words were familiar too.

Pushing her out to arm's length, Samuel took her in from head to toe, gave me a mischievous sidelong wink, and said to her, "Yes, indeed, Becky, you do remind me of your mother. She was pretty healthy too."

Becky gave him a look that said she loved him as he bent to kiss her forehead. That look seemed familiar too.

"His rifle is over in the corner," were his final instructions to Becky before he went to open the store. "Might as well give him something to do while he's sitting around here like a loafer."

When he was gone, she poured more coffee for the both of us, stopping in place when she was through. For a minute I thought she was going to pour the remains in my lap, the way she was looking at me.

"One thing it helps to be able to do in life is tell the difference from when someone's laughing *with* you and when they're laughing *at* you," I said. "Saves you from losing a lot of friends by mistake."

"Friends?" She smiled at me and I took it as an peace offering.

"Friends." I smiled back at her. It was a treaty that was

far easier made with her than with any war party on the plains. Of that I was sure. In fact, when she bent over and kissed me, I was more than sure.

We went on like that for two days, sharing little bits and pieces about ourselves with each other. Me, I found out that she talked like a teacher at times because she had been one. She spoke of how beautiful her mother was and how hard life had been for all three of them because she and her mother were who they were.

Some folks were saying that the War Between the States was over the color of a man's skin and whether or not he ought to be treated as an equal, and listening to Becky when she talked about the hard times she had endured made me understand a little better what that argument was about. She wasn't black like the slaves down south, but she wasn't of the Irish-English-Scotch extraction that so many of us were out here, either. The skin color most men out here had prejudiced themselves against was the red man's kind, and it wasn't hard seeing that in Becky at first glance, no, sir.

I reckon about the only thing she found out about me that she hadn't already learned from her father was that I was quickly falling in love with her.

Still, she tended to shy away from my approaches to her, hers to me being only fleeting kisses as the days went by. For a woman who claimed to have suffered just as much as I had, she didn't seem to want to share much happiness with me, other than that one short night, that is. If she was afraid to gamble anymore in life, afraid she could only be hurt . . . well, there had to be a way of showing her different. Fact is that by the end of that second day of cleaning my Spencer I'd come up with an idea, one that might just make her see how wrong she was about herself.

Besides, I was getting restless, and I figured that even if

my leg couldn't stand all that much exercise, well, the rest of me had to have some. And that was as good an excuse as any to look up the fellow I had in mind.

Chapter 8

His name was Jim Beckwourth.

He was as tall as Jed Smith had been described to me and he was one of the original mountain men to boot. Fact is, Beckwourth had served with Smith some thirty years ago out here. Or maybe "up there" is a better term to use. You couldn't help but feel it if not say it when you took in that oversized chunk of rock and timber that Mother Nature had laid out from the Canadian border all the way down to Mexico that Pa called the "Shinin' Mountains." You sort of had to stand in awe of them. Come to think of it, Beckwourth made me feel that way too.

His father was supposed to have been of some kind of royalty back in Ireland, and his mother was a mulatto slave. I'll grant you that wasn't much more surprising than some of the mixtures that have come out of this land and its people, but he was precisely what I figured I needed for Becky to change her attitude about life, at least out here. Beckwourth had come out with Ashley and those "one hundred enterprising young men" who had made a way into this wilderness back in '24 and set up the first rendezvous for trappers in 1825. He went on to be a Crow war chief, so they say, trapping and fighting with the best of them. He had to be pushing sixty or so by now, and that was exactly why I wanted to find him. Any man who could live that long out here and still be able to tell about it—and Beckwourth could sure do that—had to have some great stories. I was counting on one of them being the one that would change Becky's mind.

Beckwourth had come back to Denver when the gold strikes in the Pikes Peak region took place, and had taken up supplying and storekeeping with his old friend, Louis Vasquez, a noted mountain man himself. But the war had started and the Indians had taken to the warpath, and there's nothing that'll put a crimp in a wandering man's style more than being left out of a good fight. So Beckwourth had taken to doing guide and scout work for the Second Colorado Infantry. I had a notion I'd find him outside one of the saloons, spreading tall tales among those who were already scared to death of the Indian problem. Using the Spencer as a cane of sorts, I made my way down the boardwalk that morning, only to find myself wishing I could walk faster, for a crowd was gathering in front of one of the saloons a block or so away.

"What's going on?" I asked one passerby. He jerked his arm loose, a look of panic in his eyes.

"You'll see, mister, and you ain't gonna like it." It was the Indians, of that I was sure. I'd seen these people, and they had a whole different way of handling a fight with the Rebels at Glorieta Pass than they did one with warring Indians in their own backyard. You can bet on that.

The man was right. By the time I got there, at least three dozen men had gathered, passing a bottle among them while those who weren't drinking were asking questions. I eased up alongside a man who couldn't have been much older than me. He wasn't especially tall, but having as fair a complexion as he did made him stand out in a crowd of leather-skinned faces. He sensed what I was about to ask, and held up a hand to ward off the question.

"I'm just listening, friend," he said with a brief smile, "although so far I can't say as what I've heard makes much sense."

A man who could only have been one of the city's businessmen from the spiffy way he was dressed got up on the boardwalk, held up a hand for silence, and seemed to magically produce a ragged man beside him for the crowd's perusal. There were some gasps and a few longer pulls on those whiskey bottles as they took in the sight of this bedraggled individual.

"Looks about ready to drop, don't he?" the lad beside me said in a soft voice. It was commentary more than concern.

"I've seen worse." I'd felt worse too.

"Mister Carney here has just made it through to our fair city, folks," the businessman said. "And he tells me that we are surrounded, that our supplies have been cut off!!" If scaring the hell out of those folks before him was what the man had in mind, he sure did achieve his goal! More long pulls, more gasps, then a steady flow of cussing came from the crowd.

"It's the goddamn Indians!" one man yelled out, not getting any argument from the rest. "Somehow, we gotta get rid of 'em." This time a cheer went up in favor of the man's suggestion.

"Don't you worry, we'll take care of 'em." To my surprise, Leach emerged from the saloon, his arm in a sling as he took up a stance beside the businessman. I had a feeling he was about as weak as I was still feeling but, just like me, he wouldn't show it.

"Way I hear it, you ain't much good to nobody anymore, Leach," a drunken voice sounded off in the crowd. I found myself moving closer to Leach on the boardwalk, knowing full well what the next words out of his mouth would be. I reckon that drunk knew, too, because he didn't waste any time waiting for them, charging straight through the crowd and right at Leach. But the big man's hamlike fist met with the side of his head and the loudmouth rolled to the side with a heavy thud.

Trouble was, he had some friends who shared the same viewpoint and came charging at Leach too. Leach backhanded the first one, sending him sprawling, but the second one hit him in the left shoulder, where he'd been wounded, and I could see the pain in Leach's face. By that time I'd made my way along the wall to his side. The man who'd hit him was winding a fist back as far as he could to hit him again. Leach was near ready to pass out, leaning back against the wall, when I brought the barrel of my Spencer up as hard as I could into his opponent's crotch. The man sank to his knees in pain that was just as bad, if not worse, as that Leach was feeling. What made it worse yet for this yahoo was me pulling the business end of my rifle back just enough to apply some pressure to his elsewheres. If you know what I mean.

After a quick glance to each side I cocked the Spencer, too, for hell was about to break loose. Two men were coming at me, one from each direction. At least they started to come at me. The one on my left stopped dead in his tracks as that young fair-skinned lad poked his Colt into the man's gut, a mischievous dare coming into his eyes now. The one on the right had all the intention and all of the speed to bowl me over but stopped short, too, held there momentarily by a huge brown hand that grabbed hold of his shoulder. By the time he looked to see who it was that had taken hold of him, a glazed look came over his eyes and he fell to the boardwalk just as dead to the world as if Leach had laid one of his meaty fists alongside his jawline.

"Don't do it, says I many a time at rendezvous!" Jim Beckwourth said, stepping into full view from the inside of the saloon. "Liquored they get and figure to take on the world," he said in almost a comic fashion, giving a pitiful look at the man he had effortlessly felled without a blow.

"For what it's worth," my companion with a gun said, definitely speaking loud enough for the crowd to hear, "I was one of those drivers who brought that last supply train in, and these two fellas here saved our bacon, right along with the rest of those who rode with 'em. If they hadn't taken such dangerous positions as they had, I figure myself and a couple of the others might not be here today."

"Boy's right," Beckwourth said, also addressing the crowd. "Ain't no decent injun fighter who didn't have at least a couple of wounds after that set-to."

"All right, people, break it up," Glen Forbush said, making his way to the boardwalk.

"Like hell, marshal!" one man yelled, pointing to the businessman. "He said we're surrounded! Said we ain't got a way out! Said—"

"I don't really give a *damn* what he said," the marshal told him, pulling out his pistol as he spoke. "All Morris, here, is trying to do is get you to buy out his general-store supplies. Don't you people think at all?" Several of those who had protested the loudest now had sheepish looks on their faces, and as they left, so did the rest of the crowd. But something told me that what had been brought to the attention of the townsfolk might not have been all propaganda. When Forbush gave Morris a harsh look, I knew he was as concerned as I was. "You pull a stunt like that again, mister, and I'll tar and feather you before I run you out of town. Understand?"

The businessman walked away in silence.

"Never figured you'd stand up for me, Hooker," Leach

said, regaining a little of his color. It reminded me that my own leg was in some pain now too.

"To tell the truth, I never did either." I tried smiling through the pain, but it had little effect on the big man. He still had that cautious manner about him.

"You wouldn't have *really* used that rifle on that fella, would you?" He cocked a squinty eye at me.

I smiled again. "Let's put it this way, Leach. If that fella had moved, he would've had one helluva worse wound than you or I have."

"Wouldn't-a had no chillern to tell the story to either, says I," Beckwourth said, a wry grin coming to his face.

"That's so," Forbush said, "but let's try to keep the trouble in the streets down to a minimum, boys." In a hushed voice he added, "What Morris was telling that crowd isn't all that far from the truth. You four just keep it under your hat, understand?" When we all nodded agreement, he turned his attention to the young man who had helped me out. Fact is, I'd nearly forgotten about him. "And what might your name be, son?"

"Breakenridge," the boy said in a pleasant manner. "Billy Breakenridge."

"You're pretty good with that pistol, Billy," Forbush said after we'd all introduced ourselves to him. "Driving freight wagons won't get you much but shot at in this climate. You have any idea of what it is you want to do out here?"

"Right now he's gonna drink a beer with me, marshal," Leach said. The two disappeared into the saloon.

"See if you can't keep Jedediah here out of trouble, Jim," Forbush said, smiling for the first time since he'd shown up.

"I'll shore 'nough try, marshal."

When the marshal went back to walking the streets, I gave Jim a glance.

"Thanks for helping out. I appreciate it." And I did.

"Por nada, Diah. It was nothing." It was surprising how much the man could change, particularly in his manner of speech. In front of a group of frontiersmen he would put on his mountain-man drawl just like Pa had at times. But speaking privately with a body, why, you'd think he knew that whole Webster's dictionary front to back, he spoke that eloquently. I reckon that's one of the things that most people overlooked about Jim Beckwourth, the fact that he was educated in more ways than one—and most of them would likely never get a chance to find it out.

"Say, Jim, you like impressing the ladies with that talk of yours, don't you?"

He smiled. "Can't say as I ever shied away from it. No, sir."

"Why don't you give me a hand getting back to Botkin's General Store. I've got a lady friend there who needs some impressing."

Chapter 9

Becky was a bit surprised when Jim Beckwourth came into the store and walked right up to her. I'd told him what the problem was as we headed back to Botkin's, the pain in my leg still no easier to deal with. That I could handle. It was the pain in my heart that was bothering me.

I don't think she knew what to make of him at first, but when he swept off his hat like he was some fancy duke, bowed to her waist-deep, and started spouting off to her in French, why, it plumb surprised me too! Now, maybe that wouldn't have been half-bad except Becky broke out in a smile and started tossing the same kind of words back at him with the same ease!

"Well, I'll be choked on a sawed log," was all I could manage to get out, falling back on one of Pa's sayings. Normally, I don't lack for words in a tight spot if they're called for—Pa claimed none of the Hookers ever lacked for words, except maybe Guns—but to hear Becky talk broken English like she had been and then go to spouting off in French like this, why, that took the water right out of the river! They took to palavering in Spanish next, which isn't quite my long suit in languages, but when they got into sign language, I felt a bit more at home since I did know that. Trouble was I never got a chance to parlay in it.

"Look, Jim, if you want to pass the time of day, why don't you do it back there," Samuel said, indicating the living quarters at the rear of his store. "Go make them some coffee, Becky." When she had left, he lowered his voice some as a troubled look came to him. "I don't mind you holding a conversation in a foreign language with my daughter, Jim, but when you start using sign language . . . well, I just had two customers who saw it and left just a bit . . ." The sentence trailed off as he searched for the right word.

"Disgruntled?" Beckwourth offered.

"No, Jim." Samuel shook his head to the contrary. "No. Disgruntled is definitely not the word to describe it. *Hostile* is closer, I think."

He was probably right too. As the Indian raids had increased, so had the dislike of the Arapahoe and Cheyenne and, for that matter, anyone who had anything to do with them. That was why some of those good citizens had been madder than hell at Leach, me, and anyone else who laid claim to being an Indian fighter. They were depending on people like us to keep them safe and free to make their living just like the miners who depended on them for supplies, and they figured we'd let them down.

"Yes, sir, Diah," Jim said when we'd retreated to the back of Samuel's store, "you got yourself a real educated young lady. Why, she talks as many languages as I do!" That was the thing about Beckwourth. Most folks had the idea that since his skin was a shade darker than most others, windburned, suntanned, or not, he was likely a lesser person than they wee. Jim, he just kept on surprising them. He could speak what I once heard called the king's English as well as the king himself, and you had to travel some to know as many dialects of the Indian tongue as he did. Yes, you could say Jim Beckwourth knew more than his share of languages.

"I hope this is to your liking, Mister Beckwourth," Becky said as plain as day when she entered the room with a tray containing three filled cups of steaming coffee and a bowl of sugar and pitcher of cream.

It threw me! It, by God, threw me! Talking like she knew also every word Webster had put in that big thick book of his, and me just sitting there looking dumbfounded.

"Better close your mouth, boy, or you'll be collecting flies like some of those bullfrogs down on the pond." It took a minute before I realized that both the mountain man and Becky were having a laugh at my expense.

"You don't put that stuff in the coffee, do you?" I asked, still not sure of what to say.

"Sometimes, Diah," she said, taking a seat across from me. "But mostly it's manners, making it available for your guest if he or she would like some."

"Oh." Hell, you'd have said the same thing if your face was turning as red as mine was then!

Jim was smiling, thoroughly enjoying himself, when I heard a commotion outside in the store. I thought I recognized the raised voices, one of them being Samuel's. A look of concern was now on Becky's face and the smile was gone from Beckwourth's. Something told me that our visit was going to be cut short.

I was right.

"Now, wait just a minute," I heard Samuel say before his voice was stilled and the commotion became louder. By then the Spencer was in my hand, both Jim and I on our feet, ready for the trouble that seemed certain. Becky, well, she had a panicky look about her at first but was making her way to the opposite corner of the room. Truth to tell, I wasn't any too sure what to expect from her.

"Where are they?" one of them said aloud as he stomped

into the room, rifle at port arms. He had a meaner-than-hell look on his face and a voice to go with it, and I thought he seemed familiar from the crowd outside the saloon. He was soon joined by a shorter man, armed just as well as he. Out for blood is what they were.

"If *they* is *us*, mister, I'd say you found us," I said. At the same time the words came out of my mouth, the Spencer found a place in the big man's side and Beckwourth's bowie tickled a vein in the second man's throat. Momentarily, it surprised them, but they seemed determined to get what they'd come for.

"Hank, you said they was three of 'em," the first one said, nodding, his courage restored. "Said there was a squaw." The sight of Becky must have added fuel to his fire.

"That's her," the second one, who I took to be Hank, said.

About the time they started to move, my Spencer dug just a mite deeper into the first man's side. Jim pushed the tip of his knife some and a thin flow of blood trickled down Hank's neck. He must've felt the wetness running down his shirt as the fury built in his face and he glared up at the mountain man.

"Put that goddamn thing away, you nig—"

Within a fraction of a second Jim's knife was at his throat, the tip directly under the chin, another slow stream of blood emerging. It also stopped any movement of the man's mouth. Whether he knew it or not, Jim Beckwourth had just saved Hank's life.

"Seems I hear they're killin' people back east for saying that word." Hank was all ears now as he listened to Beckwourth. "Course, dead is dead, so it wouldn't make no difference ary you got your throat slit, would it?" He had a big, evil grin on his face now, Jim did, the kind I could only imagine he'd worn as a chief of the Crow nation. But when you've got your quarry cornered, I reckon you can act like that. Hank was silent as well as motionless from that moment on.

"It's bad enough we've got injuns outside the town, Hooker," the first man said to me, eyeing Becky. "Don't need 'em *inside* as well."

"She ain't an Indian, son," Jim said. "She's a lady."

"Don't make no never mind what you think she is," another voice said, this one coming down the back hallway. He stopped maybe a foot inside the room. He also had a pistol in his hand and the look of a killer about him. Cold, steely eyes said he would use the handgun without hesitation. They sent a shiver up my spine and I had one moment of doubt. "You just drop them weapons and let my friends be," he said, wielding the pistol back and forth between Jim and me. "Injun fighters, my ass. More like injun lovers. Come here, squaw," he growled.

I reckon for both Jim and me that tore it. I knew the Crow blood brother in him wasn't about to take any guff like that. Me, well, I flat didn't like pushy people, especially when they were waving a gun in my face.

Becky had that scared look again, as though she were about to break down and cry, but it was her actions that turned out to be the most unexpected of any of us in that room. The man who had entered last didn't seem like he cared a bit about what Becky might be doing over in the corner. Oh, he saw her move out of it and slowly work her way down the wall toward him all right, but he was more concerned about Beckwourth and me than a helpless Indian squaw.

Becky didn't turn out to be all that helpless.

The fireplace was built into that wall and, like most folks, Samuel had the mantel above it decorated with this and that. It suddenly felt hot in the room as my mind ran the gamut of all the foolish things the woman I loved might

do and how I might lose her at the hands of these men.
But that was a fleeting thought and somehow I knew it
wouldn't happen. There was fire in Becky's eyes as she
made that slow walk and did all the right things. About
midway in front of the fireplace, her right hand reached up
as effortlessly as though she were wiping dust from the
mantel. And the dumb bastard didn't even notice her do it!
You see, friend, when she reached the end of that mantel,
about an arm's length from the man with the gun, she had
in her hand the spare Colt Sheriff's Model that Samuel kept
up there. And that hand shot out just far enough to put the
business end of the pistol up against the man's face. Cocking it dried up the well this yahoo was pulling his courage
out of right quick.

"I don't like you or the name you called me," Becky
said. The only emotion in her voice was pure hatred. "If
I'm as bad an *injun* as you believe . . . well, maybe I'll
kill you here and now." The silence was deafening as she
paused before speaking again. "Yes. Yes, I think I will."

I do believe she would have if the sight and sound of
Hank falling lifelessly to the floor hadn't interrupted us.
The man I had my rifle on did a half right to see what was
going on, only to feel the hard whack of the butt end of
Samuel's sawed-off shotgun in his side. Then the shotgun
landed upside his head and this ruffian, too, fell to the floor
unconscious. Samuel stood there a moment, the dazed look
on his face telling me he still hadn't fully recovered from
the beating he must have taken back in the store. But by
that time I'd swung the Spencer's barrel toward the midsection of the last of the three intruders.

"Mister, you look like a fish outta water," I said with
a smile that surely displayed my confidence—and a whole
lot more. I reckon you could say I was also feeling right
proud of Becky and what she'd done. She'd proved her

worth, not only to Jim, me, and her pa, but to herself, too, and that was perhaps the most important part of it.

"I oughtta kill you here and now." Samuel was madder than hell and I don't think he cared one way or another whether the yahoo's profession was that of a killer or not. I doubted that he'd heard all that had gone on in the room, but no man likes having people barge in on him or his living quarters. And for the trouble these three had caused, I do believe Samuel Botkin could have emptied that sawed-off into the third man and no one would have blamed him one bit.

"Why, thank you," I heard Marshal Forbush say as the man turned to exit the same way he'd come in, only to be greeted by the local law and have his gun taken from him. "I'll just add this to my collection." He smiled, forcing the man back into the room. It always seemed like Forbush was having a good time at this lawman business; either that or he held one hell of a poker face through it all.

"Jim, I thought you were going to keep Diah, here, out of trouble for me."

"Oh, I did, marshal, I did," the mountain man replied with a smile. "He coulda killed these pilgrims, and just think of how that woulda cut into your poker-playing time."

"Yes, there's that," Forbush said in a thoughtful manner. "Now, would someone like to tell me just what happened here?"

After sorting it all out and bringing Hank and his friend to a feeble state of semi-consciousness, Forbush gathered up the weapons of all three and herded them off to jail, reminding me again to stay out of trouble.

"If you'll warm this coffee up just a tad, I'll finish it and be on my way," Beckwourth said to Becky when Samuel had gone painfully back to his duties in the store.

"But I thought you were going to—"

"That girl don't need no talking to, Diah," he said in that mischievous way he had. "She just needs someone like you to be there to prove herself to when it gets tougher than usual. If you ask me, she did right fine just now."

I didn't know what to make of it when Becky brought the coffeepot into the room and refilled our cups, jabbering away in French to Beckwourth again. He burst out laughing once and I thought I saw a shy smile come from her afterward. Me, I finished my coffee and tried to look like nothing unusual was taking place.

"Time for me to git," Beckwourth said, drinking the last of his coffee and rising. "Ma'am, it was a pleasure."

"You're welcome back any time you please, Mister Beckwourth," Becky said with a smile. I could tell she had really enjoyed the conversation with the mountain man despite the interruption.

"Make sure you tell him all about those plans of yours," he said from the hallway, and I had a notion those plans were what they'd been talking about.

"Mister Beckwourth," she said in that way a woman has that tells you a secret's been let loose but not to you.

"Plans?" I still didn't know what they meant.

"Why, shoot, boy, she's gonna make a decent man out of you!" Seeing the surprised look on both our faces, he gave out a laugh and departed.

That left us fiddling around with the cups and saucers for a moment, avoiding each other's eyes.

"I'm real proud of you, Becky," I finally blurted out. "You done fine this morning. Proved you'll do to ride the river with, that's for sure."

"Thank you." It was her shy voice that spoke it, but the look in her eyes told me it was what she'd wanted to hear.

"You wasn't serious about marrying me, was you?" There were a few things she had to know, and I figured I might as well spit them out here and now. "You're way too good for me, Becky, especially with all those fancy languages you speak. And I don't have much of anything to offer. No money, no land, no home to speak of. What I make in this line of work ain't going to give a lady like you the kind of things you oughtta have." I looked her square in the eye, knowing I hadn't a chance at having or deserving her, but wanting her just the same. "You wouldn't want to marry me, would you, Rebecca?"

She took my hand, rose from her seat, and in a slow, awkward manner I got to my feet too. Then she was facing me and I thought I saw that same desire in her eyes that I felt within me.

"Jedediah," she started softly, "it doesn't matter how many languages a person knows, not when it comes to love. As long as you are true to your loved one, there will be no other language you need.

"As for material things, I have no want for them. You see, my love, I have a faith in you that I believe goes right along with the deepest of loves, and I have no doubt that you will provide for me as a man does for his woman. I have that deep love for you, Jedediah, and I have had it for some time now." She kissed me gently on the lips, and smiled when we parted. "Yes, I do want to marry you."

All I can tell you is that whatever coffee was sitting there got awful cold before I stopped kissing her. Maybe that wasn't what you call a formal proposal, but it was about as close as I'd ever come to one. Hell, you'd have done the same thing if a raven-haired beauty like Rebecca Botkin had just told you she loved you.

Chapter 10

Becky didn't waste any time going to work on making a fancy gown for the ceremony, setting to it the very next day. Truth to be told, it bothered me some, for I hadn't even spoken to Samuel about the whole situation! What if he said no? What if he objected to the whole idea? I reckon it showed, too, and I don't mind telling you that the palms of my hands got downright sweaty when Samuel was the first one to notice it.

"Something bothering you, son?" he asked about mid-morning that day. Becky had driven me out of the back rooms and warned me not to return, so I'd been circulating among the customers at Botkin's, trying to look like I couldn't make up my mind, which wasn't far off. It's just that the goods Samuel stocked in his store were the furthest thing from my thoughts.

"Well, sir, uh—" I let it trail off, knowing that whatever I said would be the wrong thing.

"Oh, go on, Diah," he said in his friendliest manner, "you can tell me. After all, your pa and I go back a long ways. Why, you're almost like family around here." There were no customers in the store right then, which was good, for I had no desire to make our conversation a public one.

No, sir. But all of a sudden a strange feeling came over me, one I could only imagine must have been the same as a gopher feels when he discovers he's walked in on a rattlesnake convention. If you know what I mean.

"Samuel," I said with caution, "why is it I feel like I'm missing something?" It came to me then that his mention of family had made it all too easy for me to open up to him about what was really on my mind. And that made me cautious. There was only one way that he could know. The grip on my Spencer got about as firm as it would be if I was in in any other tight spot as I cocked a suspicious eye at the smiling man. "Mister Botkin, did Becky tell you—"

"As a matter of fact, she did," he said, cutting me off. "At breakfast this morning. Yes, indeed." The smile was still there, a knowing look accompanying it. Me, I was just standing there, feeling like some kind of fool.

"But—"

"Oh, it was nothing she said directly, son, you needn't worry about that." I could tell by his expression that he was going back in time some. "Her mother had a radiance that would come out on special occasions, Diah. Wonderful woman, she was. Becky has the same way about her. It's . . ."

"Something you know but can't put your finger on," I said, supplying the words I knew he was searching for.

"Yes. Yes, that's it."

Maybe it was me saying it for him, the way someone in a family gets to knowing how another member thinks, that made me feel a bit more at ease. Still, there was the *question* and the formality of it all, and that made me a bit queasy.

"Well, sir," I said, half choking on the words, "then you know how I feel about—"

"Don't tell me you're worried about *asking for her hand*

and all that,'' he said. The man was almost as good as Pa at interrupting a body in the middle of what he wanted to say. Yup, Pa could do that all right, for damn sure!

"Well, sir, it seemed like the right thing to do if I'm—"

"Tell me something, Diah,'' Samuel said, doing it again, only lowering his voice this time.

"Yes, sir.''

"Who was it sent you after my daughter?''

"Why, you did, sir. Pa recommended me and you—''

"Tell me something else, son.'' What the hell, Pa did it all the time too. I didn't like it, but he did it anyway. Might as well get used to my potential father-in-law doing it too.

"Yes, sir.''

"Do you honestly think that I would let anyone get as close to a woman as beautiful as Becky if I didn't *trust* them first? Especially when she's my *daughter*?'' He was looking me square in the eye, daring me to give the wrong answer. Or maybe he was daring me to give the right one; hell, I didn't know.

"No, sir!''

"Betcherass!'' He smiled and slapped me hard on the shoulder, which I took to be a positive response. "You just be good to her, son, and you'll have my blessing every day of the week.'' There's a look that a person will give you when they've accepted you one way or another, but it's a hard one to describe. All I know is that Becky's father was letting me know I was being let into the Botkin fold. "Now, get out of here,'' he added abruptly, "you're driving away my business.''

"Yes, sir.'' I turned to go.

"One other thing, Diah.'' I stopped dead in my tracks, wondering if I was about to get chewed out after all.

"Sir?''

An irritable look came over him and I knew I was in for it.

"Stop calling me sir! My daddy was sir. You call me Samuel . . . Diah." With that last his voice lowered to its normal tone again and a wave of relief swept over me.

"I'll remember that . . . Samuel." I smiled.

"Diah."

"Yes . . ."

He grinned. "Don't go looking for him unless you want to head a thousand miles east and dig six foot down."

I returned his grin. "You bet." Then it crossed my mind that we were talking about a dead man, but before I could say anything more, Samuel Botkin had terminated our conversation.

"Yes, ma'am," he said to a woman who had entered the store, "what can I do for you?"

So I decided to take a walk just to be doing something. But in the back of my mind I had a suspicious notion that the romance that had come about between Rebecca and me was the doing of my pa and hers which, if you think on it long enough, can be unsettling.

Not that I was complaining, you understand. Not one bit.

That walk I took wound up filling me with fear for the Botkins more than anything. When it was over, I had a strange feeling about Becky and that wedding dress she'd started on.

Pa tells the story of how Jim Bridger had an arrowhead stuck in his back for a couple of years and had the thing removed by a bonafide doctor back in '35, Marcus Whitman by name. The good doctor seemed awed at how little infection there was in the wound once he removed the arrowhead, to which Bridger, being just a mite arrogant as a mountain man, replied with a snarl, "Meat don't spoil in the Rockies.'' Well, hoss, taking that walk gave me the notion that Old Jim might've been right. I wasn't strutting around like some spring chicken, but the wound seemed to be healing fast enough and I wasn't feeling as strong an urge to use the Spencer for a cane as I had before. Likely it was because I wasn't paying all that much attention to the pain, which was only because I'd been paying more than usual attention to Becky.

A crowd was gathering to watch one man tack up posters every block or so, a small group of men falling off from the original group each time he moved on to put up another notice.

I stopped in front of the saloon where the fracas had taken place not a day before, following the movements of the smaller groups as they read the notice, talked briefly among themselves and scattered to the far winds, probably to spread the word.

"What do you think it is?" Leach asked, appearing beside me. I knew that, like me, he was primarily an Indian fighter and a guide, having little desire to find out when the next town council meeting or Sunday church social would be.

"Beats me. Whatever it is, though, you can bet on one thing. It's got 'em scurrying about." The start of a grin came to my lips. "You don't think the war's over, do you?"

"Hell, no!" he said with disgust. "Them damn fools back east are gonna keep throwing bodies at one another till they all die excepting Lincoln and Davis. That ain't a war, Hooker, that's politics." His voice was still deep and gruff, but the antagonism wasn't there like before. That sort of shocked me some, to tell the truth. It's just that I couldn't picture Leach as ever being all that civil toward me. Still, stranger things had happened.

"You still drinking beer?" It was about as conversational as I'd ever gotten with the man. Like I said, stranger things had happened.

"Just finished one," he said. "But if you figure you can afford the two bits they're charging for 'em, I'd go for another."

The doubts I had must've shown in my face. "Tell you what, Hooker, *I'll* buy *you* a beer. Hell, I owe you at least that for stepping in when you did yesterday."

So he ushered me into what passed for a saloon in that town and ordered up two beers. Now, hoss, August isn't what you call one of your cooler months in the Colorado Territory. Fact is, it can be downright hot. Yes, sir. And that means that expecting ice cold beer is pure horse apples, even if the sign says so.

"How's that lady friend of yours?" Leach trying to conversational again, which was not one of his strong points. But what the hell, maybe the man did have a good side to him. Maybe.

"Doing fine," I replied, sipping the lukewarm beer. I was tempted to ask why he had taken a sudden interest in Rebecca Botkin, but if the man was making amends, it would be the wrong thing to do. "Shoulder healing up? Leg's getting better on me."

"Not fast as I'd like," he said, smiling for the first time in a long time. "Reckon I just got more meat to heal up than you do."

The fellow tacking up the notices came by about then and another small crowd formed outside the front of the building. I have to admit that by now I was getting a wee bit curious as to what it was that was causing such a fuss throughout town, but I nursed that beer until I was through with it, as did Leach. By then those who had come back into the saloon were mumbling something about the governor, so Leach and I made our way outside to the now vacant area around the poster.

It was signed by John Evans all right, but it put the trouble we'd been having with the Indians in a whole new light, and I can't say as it was one that I favored. The notice stated:

PROCLAMATION

Having sent special messengers to the Indians of the plains, directing the friendly to rendezvous at Fort Lyon, Fort Larned, Fort Laramie, and Camp Collins for safety and protection, warning them that all hostile Indians would be pursued and destroyed, and the last of said messengers having now returned, and the evidence being conclusive that most of the Indian tribes of the plains are at war and hostile to the whites, and having to the utmost of my ability endeavored to rendezvous, promising them subsistence and protection, which, with a few exceptions, they have refused to do:

Now, therefore, I, John Evans, governor of Colorado Territory, do issue this proclamation, authorizing all citizens of Colorado, either individually or in such parties as they may organize, to go in pursuit of all hostile Indians on the plains, scrupulously avoiding those who have responded to my said call to rendezvous at the points indicated; also, to kill and destroy, as enemies of the country, wherever they may be found, all such hostile Indians. And further, as the only reward I am authorized to offer for such services, I hereby empower such citizens, or parties of citizens, to take captive, and hold to their own private use and benefit, all the property of said hostile Indians that they may capture, and to receive for all stolen property recovered from said Indians such reward as may be deemed proper and just therefor.

I further offer to all such parties as will organize under the militia law of the Territory for the purpose to furnish them arms and ammunition, and to present their accounts for pay as regular soldiers for themselves, their horses, their subsistence, and transportation, to Congress, under the assurance of the department commander that they will be paid.

The conflict is upon us, and all good citizens are called upon to do their duty for the defence of their homes and families.

"Now he's making sense," Leach said upon reading it, but his smile had turned back to a leer and I could almost feel the meanness coming out in him. Reading that proclamation and seeing the look on Leach's face was what made me fear for Becky that day.

"You really hate 'em, don't you?" It was all there in his eyes and I need not have asked, but I did. His expression was the same twisted, hate-filled, killing mean one I'd seen on him during the Indian attack. It was what the Mexicans called the *Deguelo,* which meant give no quarter.

"You bet I do!" The determination in Leach's voice said that if I hadn't known before, I was damn sure going to know now. "Hooker, You go out there and fight the injuns and you then come back here and you talk up for 'em every once in a while." There was a rage building in him like I'd never seen before, and the loudness of his voice was drawing a crowd.

"True enough," I acknowledged calmly. He had my curiosity up, but I was playing it cautious just the same. "That's something my pa taught me, Leach. Said he'd met good and bad of all kinds. Said—"

"Stop it!" he yelled into my face, visibly forcing me back against the wall. I'll tell you, friend, if this was how one of those volcanos spews out hot rocks and such . . . well, you can keep them. "To hell with your daddy!" he yelled again, rage pouring out of him like hot lava. He grabbed me by the shoulders and held me against the wall, his eyes big and round and just daring me to try to move.

"They oughtta be dead, Hooker! You hear me! Every damn one of 'em!" The crowd was growing, but I had a feeling that I was on my own with the madman before me. "Ever wonder why *I* don't tell no stories by *my* daddy, Hooker?"

If you've ever had something that weighed a lot pressed

up against you real slow, you'll know the kind of pain my shoulders were feeling as Leach applied pressure from his hamlike fists. Maybe he didn't know what he was doing to me, but it hurt like hell and I found myself forgetting all about my leg.

"Let go of me, Leach." I said it slow and deliberate as I brought the barrel of my Spencer up under his chin. But he didn't even notice it, for he was in a world all his own now, reliving something he'd carried inside of him for some time.

"I don't tell no stories 'bout my folks 'cause the red bastards *killed* 'em, Hooker! They killed 'em, you understand! And every goddamn one of 'em is gonna die for it! You understand!" Suddenly his grip loosened and the fire in his eyes died out. Then the rage was gone and he knew where he was and what he was doing again.

"Yeah," I said, lowering my rifle, "I understand."

"Leach." Billy Breakenridge placed a cautious hand on the big man's arm. "Come on, I'll buy you a drink."

"Sure." Billy led him off, the way you would a man who's been dazed and isn't sure where he is.

I took the opportunity to leave then, not sure I could put up with Leach in that state of mind again. Heading back toward Botkin's, I added one more worry to my list.

Something told me that where Leach and I were concerned, I'd better fear for my own life as well as Becky's.

Chapter 11

Things have a way of changing fast out here and sometimes they just go from bad to worse no matter how much faith or hope you claim to have. A week later things got worse.

As if the proclamation the governor had posted making it officially open season on Indians wasn't enough, he sent a message out a week later saying that those who lived in Denver were now cut off from the rest of civilization and were about to starve to death, if we didn't get scalped first. Not that there wasn't a good bit of truth to it, for word had it that a man and young boy had been killed by a war party no more than a day or two back. I reckon that telegraph operator's imagination was just as lively as everyone else's as he sent that message out over the wires, and it wasn't long before the governor's words had spread among the population and a general state of panic gripped the people of Denver.

"I still say you oughtta sign on for a hundred days like the rest of us, Hooker," Leach said to me one day over a drink. He'd gotten all sorts of friendly and hospitable since that day he'd spilled his guts, trying to show me how generous and kindhearted he could be. All of which might

have been true, but I wasn't having any of it. I'd pegged
him for a dangerous man from the start. Besides, from the
outpouring I'd heard the week before, I knew it would be
a cold day in hell before Leach changed his line of thought.
"They're looking for injun fighters, and you and I are 'bout
the best, Hooker. You know that. Chivington could sure
use you in that new Colorado Third he's heading up."

Colonel John M. Chivington had distinguished himself
at Glorieta Pass when the Confederates made their try at
winning the war in the West a couple of years back. He'd
proven himself to be a tough fighter, even though he was
a preacher of sorts, and was soon known as the "fighting
parson." But I'd heard Pa and Samuel Botkin discussing
the man once and went along with their belief that he had
forsaken his pulpit for a saddle and saber. And as for the
power of God, well, let's just say that Chivington had
turned it in for any kind of power he could get. Hell, there
was even talk that he might be seeking office, although few
could see this madman as a governor of our territory. He
just didn't fit.

"Why, these boys would be proud to have you ride with
us, Hooker," the big man continued.

"Not me," a familiar voice said from behind me. Over
my shoulder I could see Hank, one of the men who had
come busting into Samuel's store. He was likely passing
those cuts under his chin off as shaving nicks, but the crust
was still there from not healing as quick as he might want.
"He ain't nothing but an injun lover." Hard and mean was
how he said it, just like he had that day in Samuel's living
room.

"Some people never learn, do they?" I said to no one
in particular but loud enough for all to hear. By now I was
leaning against the makeshift bar at an angle that would
send me at him like a bat out of hell if he was looking for
trouble again.

"You better watch it, injun lover." He was looking for a fight all right; lordy was he. "You notice we don't let the likes of Beckwourth in this place. What makes you think we're gonna let you—"

"Now, ain't that innersting!" I know I wasn't expecting it, and truth to tell, I don't think any of the others were either. With the door closed you could barely see in that saloon, and there was a lot of eye straining going on right then, of that you can be sure. We all knew the voice. It was just that you had to look right hard to see Jim Beckwourth seated in a dark, dank corner. When he arose, it was slow and lumbering, the way a bear moves after waking from a long winter's nap, but you knew he was there. Moving toward us, he broke the silence that had come about when he'd first spoke. " 'Cause ary you're keeping me outta here, sonny, you're doing a *damn* pore job." A line of sweat had broken out on Hank's forehead, and it wasn't from the heat. "Ain't it a shame, Diah?"

"What's that, Jim?"

Slowly, Beckwourth moved a finger along Hank's throat, tracing the two holes his bowie had made. "Why, this pilgrim here, of course. Anyone can see he's been fighting a griz, bloodied as he be. Shame is he won't live to be old as me so's he can say what I'm 'bout to."

"Oh?" This was going to be interesting. Real interesting.

The war map that was Jim Beckwourth's forehead wrinkled up as a mean, ugly scowl came to his face and he threw Hank a one-eyed stare. Hell, you'd have thought he was some medicine man giving out the evil eye. And maybe he was.

"Ain't no one *lets* me in and out of no place, sonny. I go where I please in this country." His voice was low and soft but no one questioned what he'd said.

"Get outta here, Hank," Leach said, "you've caused enough trouble."

The man had been humiliated and he didn't like it. Still, he headed for the door, following Leach's order. Then he got a sudden case of pride and stopped, turning to give me and Beckwourth a hateful glare. "You'll pay for it, I swear. You'll pay."

The threat was leveled more at the mountain man than me. Jim sensed it too.

"Well, now, Hank, I'll tell you. I done paid for most things in my life a dozen times over, way I figure it." The kind of smile that tells you you're dealing with a man who's got the upper hand flashed across his face. That first had been pure philosophy. What he was getting down to now was business, pure and simple. "But ary you're foolish enough to try to collect, sonny, why, you go right ahead and try. Yep, you do that."

Hank, he couldn't win for losing, and the way he stormed out of there it didn't take much to figure he knew it.

When things settled down, I finished my beer and thanked Leach, saying I had to be on my way.

"But what about joining up? How 'bout coming with us, Hooker?"

"Fighting Indians is one thing, Leach," I said. "But when I'm just as likely to be fighting the man who's supposed to be watching my back"—I shrugged—"it ain't worth it. Sorry, but I'll pass this time."

Chapter 12

Hank wasn't the only member of Chivington's group who was less than qualified as a so-called Indian fighter. If what I saw for the next couple of weeks was any example of the fighting spirit of the newly formed Colorado Third Volunteers . . . well, they were much better braggarts and drinkers than they were fighters. The Indians were still a threat to us, but so far Chivington and his men hadn't shown an awful lot of accomplishment at their mission. The run-in Hank had had with Jim Beckwourth was as close as any of them had come to doing any fighting. If he was going to make a name for himself and his unit, Chivington was going to have to do something right quick to get the public's eye.

He did.

"I just wish they'd send them away from here," Becky said one day, watching the store while Samuel ate his lunch. "They scare me, they really do." The fear in her voice was anything but make-believe.

"I wouldn't worry too much, Miss Botkin," Glen Forbush said. "The federal marshal has them under lock and key now."

"That isn't much consolation, marshal, if what I've heard is true," Becky said.

"It's true all right," I said. "Sad but true."

The "they" Becky was speaking of were five members of the Reynolds gang, who had turned out to be as much a bother to the community as the warring Indians. Their leader was a former Coloradan who had taken up with the Rebels and decided to plunder the countryside where the Indians hadn't hit. In the spring they had held up a stagecoach, taking some three thousand dollars in gold dust and passengers' valuables. Word had it that there were more than twenty of them at the start, but as they moved into Colorado, the gang lost some of its men, whether by choice or through untimely gun battles no one was certain. Between being hunted by soldiers and a number of angry posses, the Reynolds gang had made itself scarce after a while, breaking up, some claimed.

From what I was hearing now, that had only been a rumor. A young lieutenant from the First Cavalry had led a company of men after Reynolds about the end of July, a gun battle ensuing one night when the outlaws' campfires were spotted. The cavalry took off after the gang. Meanwhile, the next morning a posse out of Fairplay arrived at the scene and found one of the gang members, Owen Singleterrey, deader than an empty bottle of whiskey. Now, friend, I don't know if those folks over Fairplay way were trying to claim they'd done him in or not, but they sure did let the population know that they'd had enough of the Reynolds gang. At least that's the impression I got when I found out they'd chopped Singleterrey's head off and were preserving it in alcohol for all the town to see. Gruesome but effective.

Now five members of the gang were caught by the First Cavalry and brought into Denver, and were being held in prison, awaiting the return of the United States Attorney assigned to Colorado. John Reynolds, the leader, was one of them, which made it all that much worse, I reckon.

"If you're worried about a break-in or break-out, Miss Becky, don't be," Forbush said, again trying to be consoling. "Marshal Hunt's a good man." Still, Becky seemed upset about the whole thing. When Forbush left, I tried to cheer her up some.

"How's your dress coming along?"

"Oh, it's fine, Diah," she said, smiling now like I envisioned seeing her for the rest of my life. "But don't you go back there until Papa tells you to!" I took the look and gesture to be mock warnings, although I'd long since learned that you just can't tell about the female species. They tend to get unpredictable at times. And that wasn't something Pa had told me, either.

Ever since that talk with Samuel, I'd taken notice of Becky and the mood she was in concerning our marriage and had come to the conclusion that her father was right. I didn't know what Missus Botkin had looked like, but if Samuel said she'd had a radiance about her that showed all over, well, her daughter had it too.

"You know, Becky, every time I see you I'm glad your pa sent me out to fetch you from St. Louis." I took a quick look around the store, saw that there were no customers at the moment, reached across the counter, and gave her a quick kiss. I knew it wasn't enough, but for now it would have to do.

"I see that young love doesn't get driven away by old men," Samuel said, entering from the back. "Maybe I should make my lunch hours longer."

"Now, Papa, don't you start up on me," she said, leaning over to give him a peck on the cheek across the counter. Then she was gone, leaving me with nothing but a longing look as she went back to working on her dress.

"Still trying to drive my customers away, are you, son?"

Before I could answer, Forbush came back into the store. And I don't mind telling you that the look on his face was not one I'd ever seen in a poker game. There are frowns and then there are frowns, and the one on his face now wasn't the kind that made you think he was concerned over whether or not he was going to draw the ace of diamonds to make a straight flush. It was more a sign of genuine aggravation.

"You know, marshal, someday you're actually going to come in here and buy something and I'll be surprised as hell," Samuel said sarcastically. It wasn't that he was cheap, you understand, it was just a feeling most of us had that Forbush held on to most of his money for the late-night poker games.

It was the wrong thing to say at the time. The aggravation turned to mad and the sometime marshal, sometime gambler pulled a coin out of his vest pocket and tossed it on the counter, giving Samuel a scowl.

"All right, Botkin." He was all business. "Act surprised as hell, give me as many Spencer shells as that coin'll buy, and keep your mouth shut." Then, turning to me, he said, "Are you well enough to ride, Diah, and are you for hire?"

"For hire?" I was not only curious but confused as well.

"That's what I said."

"What'd you have in mind?" I was feeling well enough, what with my leg nearly mended, but I had a notion I wasn't being let in for an easy task. Not if the look on the marshal's face was anything to go by.

"I want you to do some tracking for me."

"Why don't you do it yourself?"

"Because I've got other duties and other prisoners to watch," he said. "Besides, I can trust you."

"Since when did it become all-important that you watch your prisoners instead of your deputy?"

"Since I found out what I did half an hour ago. Believe me, it isn't making my job any easier."

That was when I found out that Chivington had made his move. Some would call it unit rivalry, some would attribute it to the huge swelled head the "fighting parson" was getting, but somehow, Chivington had convinced the federal marshal that the five Reynolds gang members, being part of a guerrilla Rebel unit, should be tried by a military commission. Forbush had wired his superiors in Leavenworth, but was informed that the commander was gone and that only he had the power to tell Chivington what he could or couldn't do with the Reynolds gang. That didn't stop Chivington at all.

"Hunt just let him take the prisoners into his custody," Forbush said, shaking his head. It was obvious that the faith he'd had in Hunt was now shaken. "Supposedly, Chivington's men are going to escort Reynolds and his cohorts to Fort Lyon for trial."

"Supposedly?" Samuel couldn't have cared less about tending store just then.

"Supposedly," Forbush repeated. "Fort Lyon is close to two hundred and fifty miles from here, a ten-day ride, nine at the minimum. Hunt says Reynolds and his men were still in chains when they mounted up and left, so I expect it'll take even longer."

"That still doesn't say much about what it is you want me to do, marshal," I said.

"I want you to follow Chivington's men. It's a fairly large force, so it won't be that hard at all. What I want to know is whether or not those prisoners make it to Fort Lyon."

"Why the concern over Reynolds and his men? You know as well as me that they ain't nothing but scum."

"I won't debate that, Diah," Forbush said. "But there isn't much use in me wearing this piece of tin"—he thumbed the badge he wore—"unless I can stand by what it means. Scum? Sure. They came after me, I'd kill 'em in a minute and go back to my poker game. But those big black books the town attorney keeps handy say a man's got to have his day to speak his piece." He paused a moment, glancing from Samuel to me. "If you ask me, those men will never make it to Lyon."

"That your gambling instinct talking, marshal?" Samuel asked, a bit more politely this time.

The lawman shrugged. "Some. But mostly it's based on fact. You see, I did some checking, and found out this Third Colorado group that's going to Fort Lyon all drew rations for the trip."

"So?"

"They didn't draw any for the five prisoners they're taking with them." When he saw the looks on our faces, he paused again briefly, then nodded. "That's right, gentlemen. Makes you kinda wonder, doesn't it?"

"Well, I'll be damned," Samuel said in awe at the prospect of what might happen.

"Most of us are, Mister Botkin, most of us are."

"You mentioned hiring me, marshal. From past experience that means I'm going to get paid. Just how much did you figure on offering?" I asked. It couldn't be much since, like I said, Forbush was pretty tight with a dollar.

"Well, let's see." He pondered, rubbing his chin. "I've already bought you your ammunition. Tell you what, Diah, I'll throw in some side meat and fix you up with a few sourdoughs to boot. How's that?" Samuel gave him a look that said everything I was thinking and more.

"Marshal," I said, "you ain't dealing with some lone wolf who'll settle for any old piece of carcass you throw to him. Why, it won't be long before Becky and I get hitched and I'll have all sorts of responsibilities. Now, how do you think I'm going to do that without a decent amount of pay for my work?''

"Reckon you got something there, Hooker. Hmm, let me see," he said, gazing off into nowhere while he mentally counted. Nodding to himself, he added, "Yeah, that oughtta do it.'' Then he stood there and smiled at the two of us like the fox who found himself the chicken house.

"Well?'' Samuel said impatiently.

"Miss Becky!" Forbush yelled out in a voice I didn't think a man his size was capable of.

"Oh! Mister Forbush," she said, rushing into the room post haste, a look of alarm followed by quick relief crossing her face. "I thought there was trouble—''

"Not from me, ma'am," he replied, tipping his hat. "I just need your attention for a few moments, if you please.''

"Why, of course.''

"I hear that you and Jedediah are about to be married and I wanted to wish you the best of everything.''

"Thank you, marshal. Thank you very much.'' She smiled at him.

"By the way, ma'am, just when is it you're planning this event?''

"December twenty-seventh," Samuel said in a most definite manner. Come to think of it, I hadn't even spoken to either of them about what date the wedding would take place. Too infatuated with Becky, I reckon. "It was our anniversary," Samuel said to his daughter, "your mother's and mine.''

"I understand, Papa," she said, taking his hand in hers.

"Well, if that's settled, you two youngsters can bank on it being the biggest one this town will ever see," Forbush said before abruptly turning to go.

"Forbush, what in the devil are you talking about?'' I asked before he could reach the door.

He glanced over his shoulder, shrugged, and smiled.

"You wanted to know what you were going to get paid for that expedition I'm sending you on, so that's it. Pretty girl like Miss Botkin oughtta have a shindig to remember."

The Botkins couldn't have said a word then if they'd wanted to. Speechless, that's the fancy word I heard used one time for having a case of tanglefoot of the tongue. Looking back, I reckon I had it too. But Forbush was enjoying the hell out of it as he turned the doorknob, opened the door, and gave one final glance over his shoulder before leaving.

"Oh, yeah, you get forty dollars in cash too."

I'd have gone after him to thank him, but I suddenly found that I couldn't move, either. Becky had a bear-hug hold on me while she kissed me. I kissed her right back too.

Somewhere in the background I thought I heard Samuel making a snide comment to a woman who had walked in on us. "Well, I never!" was her remark before Samuel growled something like how, being as ugly as she was, he didn't doubt it one bit.

Chapter 13

I was checking my possibles bag a few minutes later, when Becky appeared in the entrance to my room. The news of the shindig Forbush was going to throw for us was far from her mind now. Something was bothering her and I knew what it was. Seeing me pack that possibles bag only confirmed for her that I was going out, and that meant danger with the situation the way it was around Denver now.

"How many more times will you have to go?" she asked in a small voice. "I worry about you, you know." She tried to smile, but it was a feeble attempt.

"It's what I do, honey," I said, "just like Samuel runs his store. You get good at something out here and you make the most of it." I tried to give her some sort of meaningful look, but it didn't do much good. The simple truth was that I'd told her I didn't have any kind of a life to offer a woman. And now she was meeting her first test of whether or not she could stand being my wife. I took her in my arms, held her. "Come on, Becky, you don't need a six-gun to be tough, do you?"

"I don't know, Diah." That voice was getting smaller,

filling with fear now. "All I know is that I love you very much and that I don't like to see you ride off like you do."

"Now, wait a minute," I said, holding her at arm's length. "Aren't you the spunky young lady who got her Irish up not long ago that about *love* being the only thing that mattered to her? You're not going to back out on me now, are you?"

"I'm not Irish," she said, a ray of hope returning to her smile. "That's something I have to talk to you about."

"Sure. But right now I've got some work to do." I gave the room a once-over, not seeing anything I thought I'd need while I was gone. Hell, most of it never left my possibles bag anyway. "You think you'll be able to get by until I come back?"

She seized my hand, almost in desperation, as though it were important to keep me from leaving just then.

"Promise me one thing, Diah."

"Sure, if I can. What is it?"

"Promise me that when this is all over, all the Indian fighting finished and these desperados brought to trial, promise me that you'll find some other line of work and that we'll move away someplace where its peaceful."

If she'd been out here any length of time, she'd have known that there wasn't an awful lot of peace to be found unless you hit upon one of those old haunts in the Rockies where the mountain men trapped out the beaver and no one else besides them and Mother Nature had ever been. As for finding another line of work, well, it was going to be hard to do. Like my pa and Guns, I knew weapons and Indians pretty well but not much else. Hell, if I wasn't tracking or acting as a guide, I'd likely fill some position like Forbush did as a city lawman, but I wasn't about to tell Becky that.

I nodded. "Land's opening up, Indian war won't be much longer. Sure, Becky, I'll look into some of the other prospects when it's all over.'' She let out a sigh of relief, as though she had expected me to butt heads over it. "Right now I gotta git.''

I kissed her, grabbed up the possibles bag, and headed for the back door.

"Oh, if you want something to occupy your time other than that dress while I'm gone, ask your father to tell you about how he and my father *arranged* our romance.''

If it is possible to be excited and disturbed at the same time, Becky was that.

"You mean this whole thing was set up?'' The pot was beginning to boil and I didn't want to be there when it overflowed. Besides, Samuel needed someone to give him a hard time while I was gone.

I gave her a smile, a mischievous one, perhaps, but a smile. "Why do you think I'm leaving by the back door?''

Then I did just that.

As wide a swatch as they cut and as much dust as they left in the air, it was a wonder the Arapahoe and Cheyenne hadn't put those volunteer cavalry forces to rest before now. There's a lot of flatland between Denver and Fort Lyon, and with as big a force as Chivington had sent out, it wasn't so much a matter of tracking them as it was keeping an eye on which way the dust was stirred up a few miles ahead. Those first couple of days I rode along easily, already figuring what I could do with that forty dollars.

But it didn't turn out to be as simple as all that.

On the fourth morning I waited a bit longer than usual for the Colorado Third to move out, and when the main body didn't move at all, I decided to ride ahead and take a look-see. What caught my eye was the dust of a smaller group of men leaving on an expedition of their own. They went several miles, away from the main camp, and my curiosity being what it is, I followed them. When they stopped, I heard some yelling and rode closer to them to see what was going on. That was when everything went from being cut and dried to very complicated.

The prisoners were still in irons, just like Forbush had said they were, but they were no longer on horseback. They were now the center of attention as a firing squad was being prepared to do them in. In fact, everyone was so busy getting ready to shoot the Reynolds boys that no one noticed me amble on in atop my own horse until it was too late.

"Morning, fellas," I said in my best neighborly manner. My eyes quickly searched the crowd of volunteers, looking for faces that I might recognize. There were only two, Leach and Hank. The others I didn't know. "Gonna be a hot one, do you think?"

"Oh, that it is," a man wearing a blue coat with sergeant stripes said. This fellow, he wasn't in any too pleasant a mood. "What is it, lost your way or something?"

"No, he ain't lost no way," Hank said. "He knows right where he's at."

"That's a fact," Leach added.

"Mister, you gotta stop 'em!" one man in irons said. If he was one of the Reynolds gang, he wasn't acting any too tough now. "They're gonna shoot us! In cold blood! You gotta stop 'em!" He was desperate, that much was for sure. And if what Forbush had said earlier was correct, well, he was probably right in his assumption too. These fellows damn sure weren't looking for the nearest stream to hang a fishing pole in. Not with as much artillery as they were carrying.

"That right?" It's hard to sound casual while carrying on a conversation when a man's life hangs in the balance, but I was sure going to try.

"Move on," the sergeant said gruffly. "This ain't none of your affair."

"You know," I said, dismounting, "I never was too keen on people ordering me around. Reckon that's why I never joined the army."

The sergeant decided just to ignore me, and went about ordering the firing squad to form a line.

"Listen, I didn't do no harm to you," the prisoner said, making one last attempt. "Why should you do anything to us? Just get us to Fort Lyon. That's where you're taking us for trial, ain't it?"

"No," Hank said defiantly, "you've already had your trial, Reynolds. Now you're gonna get shot *while attempting to escape.*"

"You know, friend, at first I thought you were just a bad influence on Leach," I said, getting a mite mad my own self. "But I was wrong. You're just meaner than hell and bent on showing the whole world how tough you are. Ain't that it?"

Hank didn't have a readymade answer for that one, likely because it was the truth. Instead, he walked straight toward me, the look on his face saying he was going to teach me a lesson. But he'd already given himself away and I threw two quick left jabs to his face when he was within range. They stunned him, giving me just enough time to toss my Spencer from my right hand to my left while I swung a roundhouse that caught him on the jaw and knocked him down.

"I don't have any irons holding me back, mister," I said, giving him a hard, cold glare, "and the day ain't come that I'll take any sass from you."

It surprised me that Leach hadn't stepped in and given his friend a hand. Or maybe he didn't care for the man as much as he led others to believe. He was a hard man to figure, Leach.

"Forget your petty fight!" the sergeant, now thoroughly angered, yelled. "We got work to do here." To the others he said, "Git them horses outta the way and stand back 'bout ten paces or so." He had a certain evil pleasure in his expression, the kind that said he was going to enjoy what we all knew was coming, no matter what.

"You get over there too, Hooker." It was Hank, now on his feet, a pistol in hand, waving it toward the group of prisoners.

"Damn it! Are you hard of hearing, mister?" It must've seemed like Hank was spoiling everything for that sergeant this morning. "Now, you put that damn thing away or *you'll* be the one I stand up beside these five." Then, as some sort of justification, the sergeant added, "I didn't come here to kill an innocent man."

I moved out of the way, knowing full well what was going to take place next, and sure enough the sergeant started to give his men the order to fire. About the same time he opened his mouth, a couple of the men got down on their knees and began begging for their lives.

"You'd better think about it! You men could all go to jail for what you're about to do!" I said loud enough for all to hear.

"Fire!" the sergeant yelled, but none of the men pulled their triggers. Don't ask me why not because I don't know. Maybe each of them had signed up with this hard-core outfit only to please a friend, the way Leach had wanted me to do. Or maybe they all had consciences and felt guilty as hell. All I know is that sergeant was awful mad about that order not being carried out and he wound up giving me a brief but hellacious stare. "Someone get him out of here," he growled.

He didn't have to ask twice, for Hank was within arm's reach of me in a second, the barrel of his pistol landing alongside my head. The blow was hard enough to knock me down but not out. Stunned was how I felt more than anything. Then I heard the sergeant mumble "cowards" to himself, thought I saw him draw his pistol, knew he had when the flame shot out of the barrel and one of the prisoners fell to the ground, dead.

I had a strange feeling that I was dying, when another handgun was cocked right next to my head. It could only have been Hank, for I heard Leach say "no" to him. More gunshots rang out, and when I could see straight again, all five of the prisoners were lying on the ground, motionless. Dead. And the sergeant, Leach, and Hank just stood there, each with a matter-of-fact look about him, gun smoke slowly twirling up from their now empty pistols.

"That's it. Git them horses and saddle up, all of you," the sergeant ordered. A snarl came to his lips as he added, to himself if no one else, "Besides, we've got some celebrating to do back in town, since the colonel don't need us to ride any farther with him."

"What about them?" I heard Leach ask, knowing he meant the dead men.

"Leave 'em. Buzzards and jackals will get 'em anyway."

I was just getting up when they left. Talk had proved useless to the sergeant, who'd been purely determined to see his charges killed. If I'd made any more of a fuss than I already had, I'd have been certain to wind up alongside those five lifeless bodies my own self, and that wouldn't have accomplished anything.

The only one who stayed behind for a moment was Leach, and the scowl on his face didn't make me feel any better.

"You've run it 'bout as far as you can, Hooker," he said in that deep voice that was mean at best.

"Run what?" I asked, gently feeling the lump rising on my head.

"Your luck with me, that's what!"

"Don't yell," I said softly, wondering if my own voice would rattle the inside of my head as much as Leach's did.

"I just kept you from getting blowed to hell and gone by that numbskull, Hank. We're even now, Hooker. I don't owe you nothing, understand?"

Despite the pain I was feeling, I wasn't about to be talked down to again and I grabbed a firm hold of his shoulder as he turned to leave; firm enough to get his attention and hold him in place for the moment I needed to get my piece said.

"I never claimed you owed me for nothing, Leach. I've never made a habit of shoving stuff like that down a man's throat."

"Well, it don't matter how you slice it, it's over with now," he said, jerking his arm free.

He mounted in silence, not seemingly wanting to face me again. I had a funny notion that, as much as he'd been through, he still had some kind of soft spot in him just like Becky. He was showing it now, that he wasn't as big and tough and strong as he would have you believe he was.

"Thanks, anyway," I said, "I appreciate it."

"You're on your own, Hooker," was all he said. "I can't help you no more."

Then he pulled on his reins and was gone.

Chapter 14

"Ouch!" I said as Becky pressed a piece of ice to my head. I don't know where in hell she got ice, but I was grateful for it, of that you can be sure.

I'd ridden hell-for-leather, trying to get back to Denver before Chivington's men did so I could give Forbush his forty dollars' worth of information. Thank God there are youngsters around who don't hesitate to run an errand for you when you need it done right away. I'd dismounted at the back of Botkin's store and handed a dollar to a lad with instructions to get my horse down to the livery and have them get the damn saddle off his back, rub him down, and feed him. Me, I was certain my head was about the size of a redwood tree's girth, the hard riding not having helped its condition any, but I was also aware that the horse had worked one hell of a lot harder than I had in getting me home.

I had to only half-walk and half-stagger into Botkin's to get Becky's immediate attention, while Samuel all but promised enough candy to another lad for him to get sick on if he'd go fetch Marshal Forbush. You'd have thought the kid was making his living just waiting for requests like that to come in, for he seemed to know right where to find the lawman—and I don't mean in his office.

"What happened, Diah? What—" the marshal said when he saw me.

Ain't it just dandy when you get the hell beat out of you and someone asks you what happened? I don't know about you, hoss, but I never have gotten used to it. Hell, if they're too goddamn dumb to see what it was that happened, they shouldn't be asking in the first place.

"Feels like I ran into a mountain," I mumbled. The ice was giving me some relief.

A chuckle came from the doorway and I saw Forbush standing there. "Looks like you were so infatuated with two . . . uh, Twin Buttes, that you run into one of 'em instead of going through 'em." Becky had a confused look on her face, which is probably what prompted him to smile at her and add, "I'd bet a dollar he does it all the time."

"You wantta die young, Forbush?" I couldn't find much humor in the situation at the moment.

"You're the one looks like he nearly died young." To Becky the marshal said, "You wouldn't have some coffee, would you, ma'am?"

"Just the last of a pot."

"That'll be fine, ma'am. It'll cure his ails and serve as lunch too."

She gave him an odd look but went for the coffee anyway. I hadn't had anything to eat in the last day or so but a piece of jerked beef, so if the coffee was thick enough to be spoon-fed to me, so much the better.

"If this is what your deputies get paid, Forbush, it ain't enough," I said, rubbing the back of my neck.

"Twenty a month and found is what they get," he replied, "and they don't even earn that. Now, then, you want to tell me what happened?" If he had asked me if I'd come back only for more supplies, I do believe I would have killed him with my bare hands right then and there. I was feeling flat out miserable and, truth to tell, for one fleeting second it crossed my mind that this must be how Leach and Hank felt on a permanent basis—but without the pain.

Becky brought out a cup of coffee and I gulped some of the hot liquid down, surprised that I didn't burn my mouth. I was about to have a second go at it, when Forbush grabbed it out of my hand and walked across the room to a corner cabinet where Samuel kept a bottle of whiskey.

"You don't mind, do you?" he asked Becky. The two of them certainly were good at social amenities.

"Not if Papa doesn't."

"I'm sure he won't," Forbush said, graceful as hell. Pulling the cork out with his teeth, he poured a healthy dose into the coffee, replaced the cork, and handed me the cup like a doctor issuing castor oil to a reluctant child. "Drink this, *all* of it." When Becky's face showed signs of alarm, he added, "Old family remedy." That didn't do an awful lot to console Becky, not that I could blame her.

I'd been through a similar experience before. The memory of that nearly raw alcohol hitting the bottom of my empty stomach made me take this concoction a mite slower. Still, after a couple of good swallows the effect of the mixture took hold and I didn't think I'd be needing the ice—or as much ice—anymore.

"Now, then, Diah, just how did you get in this condition?" the marshal asked, pulling up a chair.

So I told him. All of it. Well, almost. What I left out was the part about Leach and what he'd said just before rejoining his unit. That was something that still had me puzzled, still had me wondering about what really made the man tick. I'll tell you, what bothered me about recounting that story was the fact that Becky couldn't be moved from the room. She was determined to hear it all. When I was through, I figured she'd get sick, but she only had a pathetic look of sympathy about her for five dead men she had been afraid of before. I could sense the sadness my gory story had caused her as she finally left the room.

"She cares too much, Diah. Grieving for people she doesn't even know," Forbush said, slowly shaking his head in wonder. "I hope you two move away from here after you're married."

"Why do you say that?" It was almost as if he knew of the conversation we'd had before I'd left.

He shrugged. "She's gotten used to civilization, no matter where it is she came from, Diah. And you know as well as I do that the only way we'll ever have *civilization* out here is to get rid of the killers and keep the miners out of town. And if the miners stay out of town"—again a shrug—"well, there won't be any town."

"Yeah, I know." Suddenly, what Becky had said before I left was beginning to make some sense.

"Well, you take care of yourself. And thanks, Diah, I appreciate what you did." He gave me a friendly smile, and got up to leave.

"You ain't forgetting anything, are you?"

"Oh!" The surprised look on his face didn't pass for what it was intended to; but then, he wasn't playing poker either. "Got the money over in my office." He gave me a feeble smile. "I'll have it for you first thing tomorrow."

Forbush made quick work of ducking out into the store right then, and I found myself rising to follow him. I was still in need of a good meal, but the coffee and whiskey had given me a temporary rejuvenation of the body and mind. It wasn't the money I was after either.

There are a lot of noises that you hear every day that

you take for granted and never give a second thought. That is until one way or another they make a distinct impression on you when you hear them. While Forbush was heading out of the room, I thought I'd vaguely heard something out in the street that had a familiar sound to it, and I decided to take a look-see. I grabbed up my Spencer on the way out of the back room into Botkin's store.

Through the big front window of the store I could see them walking their mounts through the streets, a dour-looking group except for the sergeant, Leach, and Hank. Coming to town to celebrate what they'd done? To let Chivington know that they'd carried out their mission? Looking for me? I doubted it. But you can bet the farm I was looking for them!

It was their horses that I'd heard coming down the street. Forbush had just stepped out onto the boardwalk and Samuel was sweeping the store when I saw them. I still had a ringing sensation in my ears and the hatred I felt for Hank now made it all that much worse.

"Here," I said, thrusting the rifle into Botkin's hand, grabbing his broom, "I'll trade you."

If he said anything, I didn't hear him. My leg still pained me some, but I was a man a-purpose that moment and it didn't matter, not at all. I walked out that door, and down the boardwalk to where an alley opened up. There were plenty of horses hitched to the rails that day and more than a few folks on the streets, all of them looking at the dozen or so men riding in now. I'd advanced a few yards on the sergeant, Leach, and Hank, when I reached the alley. Hank was on the near side, just where I wanted him. Must've surprised him when I called his name out loudly in what seemed like comparative silence.

That's when I hit him. Swung that long broom handle like I was Davy Crockett swinging Ole Betsy at the Alamo that last morning. The end of it hit him square on the jaw, and if it didn't bust that part of his face, it by God connected with a few teeth! He rolled off the back of his horse as easy as you please, and I'll tell you, friend, seeing him bloodied like that made my head feel one hell of a lot better.

"Smartass son of a bitch!" You can bet I said it loud enough for anyone within earshot. Trouble was, he was the only one who didn't hear it.

"Tut-tut, now, boys," I heard Forbush say in that prodding way he had of goading a man. "You're back in town now and that means you have to do what *I say*." He might have been talking to all of them, but it was the man who had his hand on the butt of his pistol he had his eye on. From the looks of it, I would have been dead if the marshal hadn't stepped in.

"The hell you say!" the man mouthed off. "The only one we take any orders from is Colonel Chivington!" His friends gave him a good bit of support and this fool made the decision that it was time to dance and tried following through with the first step.

He never made it.

I don't think I've ever seen anyone as fast with a six-gun as Forbush! The gunman on horseback didn't even have his pistol pointed at me when a bullet from the lawman's Colt sent the gun flying off in another direction as blood flowed from the yahoo's hand.

"I don't care if the only person you take orders from is Jesus Christ, sonny!" There was nothing violent about the way Forbush said it, not like Leach would have. But you knew he meant it. "Better get that self-righteous colonel of yours to read a bit more of the Good Book to you. *Even Jesus Christ died.*"

"Is there anything else you want, marshal?" The sergeant was having another one of those days that wasn't going his way, just like the last time I'd come up against him.

"As a matter of fact, there is." Forbush still had his pistol in hand as he spoke. "I want you and Hank here, and all the rest of you boys, out of town by sundown."

"And just why do you make that threat?" The sergeant was sounding uppity now.

"Mister, I don't make threats. You just got fair warning." A hint of a smile came to the marshal's lips as he gave me a quick glance. "Besides, I've been thinking it's time we got civilized in this town, and the best place to start is getting rid of the killers."

"Killers!" The man was outraged at the term, but it wasn't him so much as Leach that held my interest. The big man hadn't said a thing so far. The sergeant glared at me hard before addressing Forbush. "Those men were shot attempting—"

"Those men were shot in cold blood, mister," Forbush said in a mean tone for as mild-mannered a man as he, "and that don't make you any better than them! They were scum and now they're dead by your hand, *and that makes you scum*!" By the time he'd finished speaking, the whole town could hear his words. The sergeant, well, he was looking down the business end of the town marshal's pistol and no doubt feeling like he was about to meet his Maker. Forbush was spilling out his own kind of hatred now, looking like he'd never flinch or feel one pang of guilt if he pulled the trigger. "Leach, I gotta talk to you. The rest of you better take me seriously 'cause I'm not bluffing."

He wasn't and they knew it. One of them dismounted to help Hank back up on his horse. The wounded man had untied his neckerchief and done his best to tie it around his wounded hand. From the bleeding he was doing, I doubted that he'd ever do any shooting with that hand again. And maybe it was just as well.

"One other thing, Hank," Forbush said when both men were mounted and ready to ride. He knew about Hank nearly being the cause of my death on that tracking mission he'd sent me on and it angered him. I don't know if he was feeling some sort of guilt about what had happened to me or not, but Glen Forbush was full of surprises that day. For an easygoing man, he was all of a sudden giving out ultimatums like one of those fancy army generals. "I ever see you within the city limits of Denver again, I'm gonna send Jim Beckwourth to come looking for you." He was pushing the man to his limit, goading him with that gamblers' smile that said he had the winning hand. But then, Hank hadn't proved himself to be much of an adversary to anyone of late. "And when he does you in, Hank, I'm not even gonna charge him for it. I'm just gonna tell him to get a horse and toss your ugly carcass somewhere out on the plains." The grin Forbush gave me said he was just waiting for this fool to make a go for it. "Leaving you there oughtta kill off half the buzzards in the territory."

"Are you gonna take that from him!" one man spoke up. It's always easier to tell someone else how to make their decisions. But when you find your own self under the gun, well, hoss, it becomes a whole different matter.

"Yes, he is," Forbush said, clearly in command of the situation. "Now, get the hell outta my sight."

They rode on then, likely to find Chivington and report to him, but there was no doubt that they were through with Marshal Forbush. Or maybe you'd say that Forbush was through with them.

"Now all you've got to do is get rid of the miners," I said, about as impressed by what had happened as anyone else who'd seen it. We all knew that Glen Forbush was a gambler, but I don't think anyone ever figured him for being a fast gun besides. Like I said, he was just full of surprises.

"Not a chance. The town would die then and I wouldn't have anyone to play poker with anymore."

Somehow I knew that even if there was only one miner in camp, Forbush would find him and his gold dust. As long as he had a deck of cards, he'd make a living.

Chapter 15

Becky thought I was some kind of hero, although I never was sure if it was because of the tracking I'd done for Forbush or what had happened out there in the streets of Denver. All I knew was that when I got back to Botkin's store, she had a mighty proud look on her face for me. Come to think of it, Samuel was looking the same way and didn't even say anything about the busted broom handle when I handed it to him and took back my Spencer. So far I had everyone's approval for what I'd done.

The fact is that when Forbush stopped back a bit later in the afternoon, Samuel gave him a personal invite to supper that night. In the meantime, Becky heated me up some side meat and I took my time eating it while she moved around the kitchen area, busying herself with the making of supper.

"You're not hurt," she chided me once, giving me a smile and a gentle kiss on the forehead. "I can see how you're looking at me."

I shrugged, smiled. "Truth to tell, Becky, I ain't sure if it's the food or being able to see you again that's making me feel better."

"Go on," she said in a shy way, and went back to her work.

A doctor would likely tell you that it was the food that was giving me back my strength, and it probably was. But there's something about the way you feel when you've returned to someone you care for that . . . well, I reckon you'd have to call it nourishment for the soul. Works as well as food any day. I could remember Pa trying to explain the feeling each time he'd return to what he called the "Shinin' Mountains." For my brother, Matt, it was likely the discovery of a new long gun to test out; with Glen Forbush it was almost certain that it was a new poker game. I'd heard Pa, Matt, and Glen each describe that love like that of returning to a good woman; how you knew she'd treat you right when you did. The difference was that I had come back to the real thing, to a woman I loved more than anyone else in this world, and only she knew how good it felt to be back in her presence. Oh, the food had a good bit to do with me regaining some of my strength, but it was the sight of Becky walking around that afternoon that lifted my spirits and made me feel a whole lot better. The bandage on the side of my head didn't make me look all that good, but by the time Becky was setting the table and Samuel had poured Forbush a drink, I wasn't complaining at all.

The marshal was praising Becky for the meal long before she dished it up, but it was well worth his compliments. I could think of a hundred men who would have married Becky for her cooking that night alone, even if she had been uglier than sin and as mean as the devil.

"Chivington is going to get away with those murders, Diah," Forbush said near the end of the meal. Up until then it had been what you call social amenities that we'd all gone through, but I reckon the marshal knew that I was a bit more than eager to find out what would happen because of my discovery. After all, murder was murder, and one way or another someone had to pay for it. It was the law, not just of the land but . . . well, it was the law. Hell, I'd heard Forbush say it often enough.

"Why?" This from Samuel, who seemed to be taking a new and renewed interest in his future son-in-law's health.

"To start with, Chivington has declared martial law, which means it's his show and he can run it any way he wants. Second, I can't get the federal marshal interested in taking on a bunch of ruffians that are being backed by our fearless 'Fighting Parson.' For right now there's simply nothing I can do." He gave a hopeless sigh and I could tell he knew he was fighting a losing battle. By referring to a man I knew he once had a good deal of faith in by his title rather than his name, I also had a notion he'd lost a friend. "But there is one good piece of news."

"What's that?" Samuel again, more interested than ever.

"Ned Wyncoop is bringing three chiefs from the Arapahoe and Cheyenne tribes here to Denver to parlay with the governor. Seems to think there's a chance of peace yet."

"Waging peace always seems to depend on how fast winter is setting in and how scarce game is for the tribes hereabouts." If he was indeed taking an interest in my health, Samuel was also becoming the skeptic that many other townfolks had turned into long ago concerning the Indians.

"Never can tell," I put in. Pa said never to discuss religion or politics because it was one of the surest ways in the world to lose a friend, a bet, or your life. And I don't mind telling you that the older I got the more I was finding out what my Pa knew that I didn't. Anyway, I'd also discovered that most anything you wanted to discuss about war—Between the States or Indian, take your pick— was tied to politics, so I just stayed away from talking about it.

Becky didn't say much of anything about the subject, sitting there and acting more as an observer than a participant. I don't know about the others, but that lack of conversation on her part sort of bothered me. After all, she had done a good deal of talking to me about the Indian; why not stand up for him now?

Conversation sort of dried up after that, and it wasn't long before Forbush was checking his pocket watch and making excuses for leaving—likely some game that was scheduled to start shortly. Still, he made it known how he felt.

"Only one person can cook better than you, Miss Rebecca," he said, rising from the table, "and that is my mother."

"I'm flattered," Becky replied, and she truly was.

"No, ma'am," the lawman said, "you're an excellent cook." Then, in a move that surprised all of us, he bent down and kissed her cheek. In a smile that was almost fatherly, he said, "If you ever get tired of cooking for these two yahoos, you come and see me. I wouldn't mind having a meal like this on a regular basis."

He bid us good night and was soon on his way.

We cleared the table and got everything set aside, me thinking that I'd be able to have a few minutes alone to Becky. Like I said, I'd been watching her all afternoon. But just as she picked up the coffeepot, the evening took a new turn.

"Don't throw that out just yet, Becky," her father said. She looked at me but I could only shrug, unsure of what the senior Botkin had in mind. Sensing the confusion, Samuel added, "I think it's time we had a family talk."

"Certainly, Papa. Take a seat in the living room, you two, and I'll bring some more coffee."

I was about to sit down on what served for a couch, when Samuel gave me a stern look, shook his head, and nodded toward the wooden chair located across from the couch. Apparently I wasn't to sit with my bride-to-be during this "family talk," whatever it was. Not that I felt edgy about it, you understand. More curious than anything, I'd say.

"There, Papa," she said, setting down a tray of three steaming cups of coffee. Not the cream and sugar, as she had done that day Beckwourth visited. Just the coffee. But then, maybe family discussions in the Botkin household were informal. I didn't know.

"The first thing I want you to know," Samuel said in a voice that matched the look on his face, "is that for a day and a half after you left, I played *hell* with this girl trying to explain how Black Jack and I were supposed to have set up this wedding of yours."

"Oh, Papa," Becky laughed, her small, soft hand not quite covering her mouth. But her father still had a serious look about him, and it was trained on me.

"Son, do you realize that if I was a butcher, you would have been so much meat hanging up in the store window? As it is, you're lucky I haven't put that rifle of yours up for sale—yet.

"The second thing I'd like to say"—here his frown softened into a smile—"is that I'm glad you made it back in one piece."

Silence reigned while we all sipped at our coffee.

"Is that it?" I finally asked.

"Noooo, not quite," Samuel said. "There is one other thing." He thought for a moment. "How should I say it? *Heritage.* Yes, that sounds like an apt phrase. We have to discuss that."

"I see." Suddenly, it all seemed quite clear. "You want to talk about Becky's Indian blood." Might as well get it right the first time and let them know I wasn't afraid to talk about such subjects. Hell, Pa did it all the time.

"Precisely," Samuel said with a brief smile. "But tell me something first, Diah."

"Sure."

"What was the name of the tribe that did in that mountain man your daddy named you after?"

Chapter 16

It was mid-September before those chiefs made it to Camp Weld and talked with Governor Evans. They were looking for peace all right, but from what I saw of it the governor wasn't any too interested in much more than reminding them that there were one hell of a lot of "depredations" that had been done to the white man by these particular tribes.

Of course, after that talk I'd had that night about "heritage," as Samuel had put it, I had a whole new outlook on what was happening to the Cheyenne and Arapahoe. Yes, I'd learned a whole lot that one night about man and his prejudices and how much we all take for granted. That was one thing I hadn't learned from Pa, for he had a good many personal dislikes of his own that he'd voice any time he pleased and to hell with the rest of the world. But that was Pa and you can bet I sure wasn't going to try to change him. What Samuel and Becky had done that night is put a lot of faith and trust in me with the story they told. They had opened up a lot more, I got the feeling, than they had ever done for anyone else. And that took guts for Samuel. Becky, well, I got the impression as the night went on that she knew I'd accept her for the woman she was, no matter what her story or heritage turned out to be.

Having that talk also made me realize that it was time to stop trying to live up to the reputation of Jedediah Strong Smith, for whom I'd been named, and concentrate on making my way in the world as Jedediah Hooker. I'd always had the thought in the back of my mind that I had to be as strong and tough as Jed Smith had been or I'd be a miserable failure. There was always the fear of letting down Pa or my big brother if I didn't come out of a fight as king of the hill. Well, hoss, that all changed that night. Oh, there'd more than likely be a fight the next time I met up with Pa or Matt, between me and one of them, or both. And I could tell you just how it would start too. One of the two would ask me if I'd lived up to Jed Smith's reputation since the last time I'd seen him—just like they *always* did—and I would start breaking some bones, by God!

No, sir, you could save Jed Smith for those fancy fellows who did all the writing of the history books about how this land got settled. Me, I'm Diah Hooker, doing my damnedest to make my way in this land. And devil take the hindmost! How's that for determination?

"Did you hear that?" Forbush asked, standing by me as the crowd of volunteers watched the proceedings. "He's passing up a chance to use those Cheyenne and Arapahoe to get rid of the Sioux and all the rest! I can't believe it!"

"What? I didn't hear you." I'd had other things on my mind.

The governor was sitting there parlaying with the Indian chiefs, the whole audience waiting to hear the interpreter's words.

"Carson is making use of the Utes down in the New Mexico Territory," the marshal said in a frustrated voice. "Used 'em as scouts to hunt down the 'Pach and Navajo last year. You'd think Evans would try the same thing."

The Carson he mentioned was another former mountain man holding the same stature as my namesake. He was Kit Carson and had been in charge of the Indian campaign against the Navajo and Apache to the south of us ever since this fool War Between the States began.

"Makes sense, I reckon. Why do you think he passed over the opportunity?" I said.

"If you ask me, Diah, the governor's been listening too much to Chivington. They're out to kill 'em all off, every Indian they can." For a gambler, I was continually surprised of late at the knowledge Forbush had of what was going on or might be going on—or could be going on. His suspicion of what would happen to the Reynolds gang when Chivington's men escorted them to Fort Lyon proved to be deadly accurate. Fact is, he was getting me real curious about such predictions.

"How do you know that?"

"Talk," he said, walking away from the crowd. Apparently, he was satisfied that he'd seen enough. "You see, Diah," he said, smiling, "you people all think I sit back at one of those tables, playing poker, making money hand over fist, while the whole town is going to hell in a handbasket. But you're wrong.

"You'd be surprised at how much you can learn in one of those games. Miner comes in and figures he's going to distract you by holding a conversation while you're holding your cards, so he starts talking about his claim, the Indian situation, anything." The smile broadened. "Trouble is, he gets so caught up in the conversation that he's the one gets distracted, and I've still got a pat hand. No, son, sitting at one of those tables is sometimes as good as talking to the town gossip."

As it turned out, those chiefs agreed to bring in all of their captive whites in exchange for meeting Ned Wyncoop, a young career officer in the army, down at Fort

Lyon to set up arrangements as to where they'd be winter-
ing this year. When I heard that, I got to wondering if
Samuel wasn't right about the tribes suing for peace when
they figured wintertime was a-coming. Fact is that it did
start to cool off not long after that.

The peace negotiations put a real damper on Chivington
and his Colorado Third, who were now being called the
"Bloodless Third," not having gotten into any real honest-
to-goodness fight with the Indians they'd thought they'd be
confronting. And in a way it all seemed to fit, for as the
months went by, the "hundred dazers" of Chivington's
group still showed little promise as real soldiers in a cavalry outfit. Toughest-talking and hardest-drinking fighters
you'd ever seen, as Pa would have put it. But that was
about all.

By the first part of November, Lieutenant Wyncoop had
been replaced as commander of Fort Lyon by a Lieutenant
Anthony. We heard something about Ned being too favor-
able to the Indians. Likely, it was just politics, but the
interesting part was that this new commander was looking
to make favor with Chivington, and that meant being tough
with the "savages" he was dealing with. So what he did
was tell Black Kettle and Left Hand and the rest that it
would be a while before he'd be able to get word from his
commander about the peace agreement and told them to
move to the Sand Creek area north by east of Fort Lyon
some forty miles. The whole maneuver, in Forbush's opinion, was to get the Indians away from the fort. Lieutenant
Anthony, it seems, wasn't as trusting of the Cheyenne and
Arapahoe as his predecessor had been.

In the meantime, I had been doing a variety of things
which ranged from helping out Samuel with his store to
sitting in on some of those poker games Forbush was so
good at. I didn't win an awful lot, but I did find out what
he meant about gathering up information about what was

going on. Why, the way some of those miners gabbed on, you'd have thought it was a Sunday church social they were attending instead of a poker game. One of the things I found out was that Black Kettle and his people were living off buffalo while they waited for an answer from Lieutenant Anthony about the peace agreement.

That set me to thinking I might be able to get some money by trading for the skins—which seemed highly unlikely, what with winter setting in—or shooting a few of the big beasts myself before they were all gone south for the winter. Hell, I'd give the meat to the Cheyenne and Arapahoe if I could bring the hide back here to Denver to sell. The reason I gave everyone that I was going to ride out there was that I was trying to make some money to set aside for the wedding and after, a man having to take care of his woman and all. But the real reason was that I didn't think I could stand much more of this civilization, as Forbush had put it.

"Are you sure you want to go?" Becky asked. From the way she said it I knew she'd miss me as soon as I walked out the door.

"I have to, honey," I said, taking her in my arms. "If I sit around this town much longer, why, you're liable to have a husband-to-be who's gone 'round the bend." I tried to make it sound funny, but she knew better than that. For having been born where she was, Becky had adjusted right well to an upbringing in the city. Hell, St. Louis was a big place, had been around for a couple hundred years they said, while Denver was just starting out. Still, I didn't think I could stand this kind of city life much longer. One thing was certain—when we got married, Becky would get one of her wishes, that being that we'd move away to some other place.

"Then hurry back," she said after kissing me. "I think I'll have a surprise for you by then."

We were standing out back of the Botkins' place, as we'd taken to doing in the evenings, talking while we watched the sun set and the stars come out. Our nights had grown shorter and shorter, but Pa had taught me a good deal about respecting nature and what he called Mother and Father—Mother Nature and Father Time.

I never did mention it to Becky or anyone else, but I had the strangest feeling at times when we were out there. But then, maybe it was just the weather. Hell, everyone else blamed any and every thing on it, so why shouldn't I.

Chapter 17

I couldn't help but wonder what it was that Becky had in mind as a surprise for me upon my return. Showing me her new dress? Something she'd made for me? I didn't know, but it stuck in my thoughts as I headed for the Sand Creek area. Come to think of it, all I had on my mind was Becky and our wedding day. Believe me, hoss, Christmas wasn't going to be anything this year compared to our wedding! No, sir.

Mind you, now, that Spencer is no buffalo gun, but it'll do in a pinch if you can get close enough to your prey, and that's exactly what the Plains Indian had been doing with his bow and arrow for a long time now. When I first got out there, I killed some game with a few of the Cheyenne warriors—a practice that seemed a mite risky at first when you consider that not long ago I may well have been shooting at one of them—and got to know these plainsmen better. But mostly it was being out in the open spaces again, not confined by any limits, that made me feel alive again.

A few days after I arrived in camp a guide known as John Smith showed up with two friends, his Indian wife, and their son, Jack. With him he brought a freight wagon loaded down with trade goods, apparently set on doing the same thing I had in mind but on a larger scale. He managed to get what he had come for, trading off all of the goods for some hundred buffalo robes, three ponies, and a mule. But that wasn't the only reason for his visit.

"Major Anthony says he wants to know how many Indians are here at Sand Creek," he replied when I asked about his mission. "Wants to know just how friendly they are to the whites, but seeing you here and still walking around, they must be sincere 'bout leaving the warpath."

"They've been friendly enough toward me," I acknowledged.

Later on I asked him about being married to someone who wasn't his own race, specifically his Indian wife. It was a chancy thing to do, for some men would tear your heart out if you asked them about that subject, but even though I didn't know him that well, Smith seemed like a level-headed man.

"There's prejudice, all right," he said, "but you gotta take that into consideration when you get hitched, I reckon. It ain't something that goes away overnight, so you gotta be able to handle it if you plan on making a go of it."

I thanked him, saying I thought he was doing right well at it, what with the boy he had and the woman still with him. Fact is it made me feel that much more confident that Becky and I could survive it all. I thought about Becky all that night, figuring that after one more day or so I'd head back to her. Hell, it was only one more month before we'd be officially married, and the way I was feeling, why, getting through one more month of Forbush's "civilization" would be a breeze.

We were up at daybreak the next morning, eating breakfast, when an old woman stuck her head in the lodge and said something about "a heap of buffalo coming."

"Won't have to go to them today," I said, making a

joke of it, because I could hear the rumbling sound in the distance too.

It was only a minute later that a Cheyenne chief entered the lodge with news that there was a large band of soldiers headed toward the camp. He wanted Smith to go and find out what they wanted. Every once in a while you get a queasy feeling in your stomach that tells you things aren't right. Not that I was going to upchuck my food, you understand, but I was suddenly getting that uneasy feeling in the pit of my stomach.

"Your commander say he figured on heading this way?" I asked Smith, just to be saying something while a whole passel of thoughts raced through my mind.

"Not that I know of," was his reply as he got up and left. He sent his son to get a mount for him, but I could see that the herd had already been cut off from the village. From the gunfire now taking place, I could tell we were under attack and that we were stuck on foot. Or maybe I should say that at least this village was under attack.

Smith must've figured that having a hat and a blue soldier's coat on would keep him from being fired on, but even if he was waving a white flag he couldn't stop those bloodthirsty cavalrymen riding into camp. And I knew they were bloodthirsty, for once they got within range I recognized them.

It was Chivington's Colorado Third with the madman himself at the head, yelling for his men to take no prisoners. I'll tell you, hoss, seeing what looked like the entire one thousand of them coming at me . . . by God, it scares you! But it also made me mad.

Black Kettle had emerged from his tent, yelling for everyone to stay calm, although it didn't seem to do much good. The Indians were in a frenzy, not knowing which way to turn. White Antelope had gone out into the clearing and stood in the open before the whole charging mass of the "Bloodless Third." At first he ran around, waving his arms at the approaching soldiers, but then he simply stood stock-still, his arms folded before him. Whether he was doing it out of defiance or to show that he bore no arms, well, I don't think anyone will ever know. They killed him where he stood and kept right on a-coming, shooting pistols, rifles, and a variety of weapons in between. Some of those so-called cavalrymen recognized John Smith out there, but one of them yelled out, "Shoot the old sonofabitch; he's no better than an Indian," and started firing at him.

Black Kettle had hoisted an American flag above his lodge, with a white flag below it, and was still out there in front of it, trying to calm everyone. Grapeshot and cannon fire now filled the air as Chivington's men entered the camp, guns blazing. One of the men who'd come with Smith climbed on top of the wagon and tried waving a white flag himself, but there was too good a chance of dying of lead poisoning up there and he was soon out of sight.

Since I'd arrived I'd noticed only a few warriors in the camp, most of them being the ones who had gone hunting with me, and they were friendly enough. The rest of the camp was filled with old men, women, and children. Right now they all had that terrified expression on their faces that reflected the questions in all of their hearts: What's going on? And why? If there had been time, I'd have told them, but there was no time.

"People," I mumbled under my breath, still as surprised and horrified as they were, "you are about to be annihilated."

An Indian woman ran into me, and was about to clutch my arms, when a bullet struck her in the back and forced her into me that much harder. I thought I felt the bullet tickle my side, but as she fell to the ground I couldn't tell whether it was my blood or hers on my jacket.

That was when I got really mad.

Some of Chivington's men had dismounted and were having a grand old time of it, going from one lodge to another to see who they could find while those warriors who did have arms of any sort made for a stream above the village, taking shelter behind its banks. But they were no match for the firepower of Chivington's maniacs. It was when the lead started flying in my direction that I forgot about them and took stock of my own situation.

Part of those bullets were overshot by some riders who'd taken aim on a man who'd come to John Smith's rescue, or at least tried to. He was riding in to pick up Smith when some shots felled his own mount and him with it. He didn't do any moving when the horse went down, so he was either stuck beneath it or dead. In either case, he was too far off for me to be of any use to him at the moment without getting killed my own self.

Instead, I saw a member of the Third reach out beside a lodge not far away and grab up a young boy who couldn't have been more than six or seven years old. With a strong hand around the boy's throat, he held him in place while he pulled down his britches. I don't know what the fancy, civilized word for it is in Webster's, but what he had in mind wasn't nothing close to natural!

''Bastard!'' I yelled at him, not caring a bit that he was a white man as I took dead aim on him and put a bullet between his eyes when he turned my way. He looked about as surprised as the rest of us when he died, but it didn't do the boy any good. Someone else's bullet found his chest, and he fell beside the man who had tried to rape him, just as dead.

I moved carefully between the lodges, not sure who I'd come upon or what I'd find. Yesterday I had been recognized as a friendly visitor to this Sand Creek village, but for all I knew now, I could be killed by either red man or white. I'd heard that Billy Breakenridge had joined up with the Colorado Third, but I figured he'd be about the only one I could count on to be friendly. Maybe that was why seeing him when I turned a corner froze me in my tracks.

"You!" He recognized me right off. The face was still craggy and the voice mean, but a mad sort of pleasure came over him as he spotted me. "They said you'd likely be here." He was bringing his pistol to bear on me, when my Spencer went off. The slug tore into his gut, knocking him backwards and to the ground. The sergeant in charge of the Reynolds killings was now about to meet his own death. But he was still determined to get the best of me. "Can't stop us now, Hooker." He leered, a sickly look crossing his face. "You didn't think the injuns down here was the *only* ones we was going after, did you? They're taking her right now." His smile said I was about to hurt worse than any bullet or arrow could, and he was right.

Her? It could be only Becky he was speaking of! And "they" could be only Leach and Hank. I hadn't seen them so far, but I could be wrong. They could be right behind me, ready to blow my brains out. But that didn't matter; right now I had to know what harm was coming to Becky. I dropped to one knee, putting the pressure of the other on his chest just enough so the pain showed in his face.

"What are they doing to her!" I demanded, grabbing a fistful of shirt and shaking his head.

The pain must have been excruciating for the man, but he held up under it well, doing his best to show me he had won. I decided then that what he needed was a bit of fear put into him, so I let go of the shirt and pulled out my bowie.

"You want to laugh, mister? I'll give you something to laugh at." Slowly I cut two lines down his throat, each about an inch apart from the other. Cutting away enough to grab a loose bit of skin under his chin, I grabbed it and yanked it down a mite. He let out a yell, but it was no different from a hundred others I was hearing now, so it didn't matter. "You ain't laughing, sarge," I said. If it was sadistic and mean, you can bet your ass it was the way I felt. Or perhaps it was seeing the madness in my own eyes that put the fear in him. I didn't know or care.

When he wouldn't talk, I wanted to kill him right then and there, slit his throat from ear to ear, do to him what he and this lousy bunch of drunks were doing to Black Kettle's people. But something inside me stopped me then, something that said if I went that far . . . hell, I'd be no better than they were.

"To hell with it," I growled, "I've got a lot to do today." I left him that way, dying in his own fear, in his own blood.

Blood was blood and dead was dead and there seemed to be a lot of it going around that day. Us Hookers are strong on family ties, and even if Becky wasn't yet a Hooker, she was about to be and that was good enough for me. I had to find a horse and get back to Denver. I had to get back to Becky before—

"What's going on here?" a rider said, reining in beside me. He glanced at the sergeant, then at my bloody knife. "Did you—"

"I need a horse, mister," I said. By then my rifle barrel was pushing into his gut. "You can give it to me peaceful like or you can die trying to keep it. Don't make no never mind to me at all." Whatever bluster he had went out of him and he dismounted.

I was in the saddle as fast as I could get there, losing sight of him only for one second. But it was one too many and when I threw my leg over the saddle I felt the bullet enter my leg before I heard the report of the pistol. I do believe he would have shot me again if he'd had the chance. I didn't give it to him.

The Spencer came around, and for the second time that morning I shot it one-handed. The bullet went high in his chest and he fell to the ground.

"Sonofabitch!" I yelled, more at the wound than him. "Got hit there before." I don't mind telling you I was getting pretty goddamn tired of getting shot at that day. Damn tired! I levered another shell into the rifle, took aim, and shot the man right above the kneecap, knowing that the bullet had struck the bone by the look on his face.

"Why don't you kill me?" he said, almost begging for it.

"No. I want you to live, mister." My words puzzled him. "Someone's got to regret this day as much as I do . . . and feel the pain it's caused. No, I want you to live to regret it."

I'd never seen anything like it before. It was wholesale slaughter that should never have taken place. But then, there were a lot of things that should never have taken place. I should never have left Denver. I should never have left Becky's side. Maybe I should never have fallen in love with her. Maybe . . .

All I could hear was the dead sergeant's smug voice saying that they had taken her. All I could see was that smile on his face that said he'd finally gotten back at me in the best possible way. All I could think was that maybe the black-eyed, raven-haired beauty I'd fallen in love with might not be able to tell me about the surprise she had planned when I got back.

Chapter 18

I wouldn't have stopped if it hadn't been for Billy Breakenridge. And if I hadn't stopped, I might never have made it back to Denver. Must be the blood that gets to flowing through your system when you get fired up that makes you bleed like a stuck pig when you get shot. I don't know. All I know is that Breakenridge all but rode into me as I headed out of camp.

"You don't get that wound took care of, Hooker, you'll be as bad off as the rest of 'em lying on the ground hereabouts." I was so filled with hatred, so filled with fear, that the wound seemed secondary to me at that moment. Still, the man had a point.

"Got anything to kill the pain?" I wanted to get it wrapped up and get out of there as fast as I could.

"No, but Lieutenant Soule and his men will have a medic with them," he replied, motioning toward what looked like a company of soldiers, perhaps the only company who had yet to partake of the slaughter taking place in the Indian village.

"Ain't you going to get yourself part of the gore and the glory, lieutenant?" I asked as one of his men tore apart my pants leg and doctored me up some. It was a clean

136

wound, the bullet having passed through the fleshy part of
the calf, but I had a notion those muscles and nerves of
mine were going to need a whole lot more time to heal
than the damage from the arrow wound had. Hell, I hadn't
completely healed from that wound yet!

"No," the young officer said without sounding at all like
the self-righteous types I'd run into so far. "The poor devils don't deserve this, not at all." Seems he'd refused Chivington's order of sending his men down into what had fast
turned into a massacre more than a battle. It was doubtful
that he'd win much favor with the "Fighting Parson," but
I had to admire the man for taking a stand against the mad
colonel when few others would.

"I tend to agree with you," Billy said. "Coming into
this thing, I wasn't sure what to expect, but after that first
wave of riders and what they started doing . . . well, I just
ain't got the stomach for it."

"Thanks for the help, friend," I said to the man who'd
fixed me up. "It don't feel any better, but it oughtta do
until I can get to Denver. Much obliged."

"Need any company on the way back?" Breakenridge
asked. "I've had enough of this fiasco."

"Fine with me. Just don't expect me to take my time
getting there."

The lieutenant and his men were easing their way down
the banks of the river as the rest of Chivington's men continued to pot-shot the few braves who were making a stand
of it.

I rode hell-for-leather trying to get there, hoping against
hope that I'd be in time. I had to be in time to save her
from Leach and his crowd. I had to!

Billy said Chivington had gone the forty miles from Fort
Lyon to Sand Creek overnight in some sort of forced-march
style. That meant the horses weren't in all that good shape.

But if it meant riding my mount into the ground to save Becky, I'd do it. I'd do anything for her.

My leg hurt like hell now, but all I could think of was getting back to Denver. Samuel wasn't about to let anyone take his own daughter away from him, so if they did try, I knew that there would be a fight.

We stopped twice to let the horses blow and get some water while we chewed on jerked beef. A hot meal would have been better—one of Becky's hot meals to be exact—but you make do with what you have, so we did.

It was late afternoon when we arrived in Denver. I think my horse would have died if he'd had to go one more mile. Truth be known, if the situation hadn't been what it was, I think I might have been in that state too. It was November 29, you understand, so it was nowhere near summertime weather.

"I'll get these to the livery," Billy said, taking my horse as I dismounted and made my way into Samuel's store.

All I had to do was see a stranger behind the counter when I entered and I knew something was wrong. The first thing I found myself doing was flattening my back against the wall and sticking my rifle out at the fellow behind the counter.

"We're about to close," he said timidly.

"Where's Samuel Botkin?" I demanded. "And Becky. Where's Becky?"

"You don't . . . really want to . . . know, do you?" I'm not sure if it was the look on my face or hearing that heavy hammer cocked on my Spencer that scared him, but something did.

"Better believe it."

"Mister Botkin is back there," the squirrelish little man said, tossing his head toward the rear.

"What in the hell happened to you?" I asked when I made my way to Samuel's bedroom. The doctor was at his bedside, finishing a patch-up process on Samuel's head and chest. Botkin didn't look to be giving him much help in getting the job done.

"That horde you tangled with out in the street after you came back from tracking for Forbush is what happened to me, damn it!" he exploded. Upset wasn't the word to be used to describe Samuel Botkin at the moment. "And the doc's trying to get me to stay in bed!" Samuel attempted to prop himself up on an elbow, as though to get out of bed, but he was too weak to do even that.

"Here, son, you'd better take a seat," the doctor, an older man, was saying to me. "You look a bit peaked yourself." He handed me a healthy dollop of whatever it was that Samuel kept bottled up in the corner of his living room, that was now on a makeshift nightstand beside his bed. "Sip this stuff easy."

"I know." I took his advice for the moment, the edge of Samuel's bed feeling mighty fine compared to the pressure I'd put on my leg getting from the front door of his store to back here.

Apparently a band of men Leach had been with had broken into Samuel's store and beaten him into unconsciousness that morning. The doctor thought Samuel had a concussion and knew for sure that he had several broken ribs.

"The damn fool needs to stay in bed. But he insists that he has to get out to go look for his daughter. Why, if one of those lungs punctures, he'll have pneumonia in no time at all!"

"Listen, Diah, they took her!" Botkin was desperate now and I couldn't say as I blamed him. Might've been his daughter, but it was my bride-to-be they'd taken! "They took her and he won't let me go out to look for her! He knows where she is, I tell you! Knows what they've done! You've got to find her! For me, for us!" I finished that drink in one gulp, knowing that it would kill the pain, at least for a while. Then I grabbed the doctor's elbow and guided him out of the room while Samuel lay back down and the energy seemed to drain from him as the tears flowed down the sides of his cheeks.

"I'd wager that leg wound needs tending to, son."

"Couldn't be more right, doc. But something else needs tending to first." I turned him around so he faced me, so he could see the pain I was feeling that had nothing to do with a gunshot wound to the leg. "Now, doc, I want to know where Becky is." I'd never talked harder or meaner in my life. "If you know where she is, where she got took, then I gotta know. 'Cause if I don't find her there . . . well, doc, *you're* gonna be the one who needs a doctor."

"Two blocks down the street." He said it as though ashamed of having admitted it. "But you won't like it."

"I'll give you a hand," Billy said when I made it outside the store and told him where I had to go. We got there quicker than I ever would using my Spencer for a crutch. I was oblivious to the cold and the wound and the pain. Right now I had to get to Becky.

The doctor was right, I didn't like it.

A small crowd had gathered around the millinery store and was gazing in the window. Not just the local women, but a lot of men too. But then, they weren't looking at any normal display.

Jesus Christ couldn't have been nailed to a cross better. The mannequin had been replaced by jagged pieces of wood that somehow held Becky up for all to see. She had on a wedding gown—was it hers?—but it was no longer white. It was blood-red from the scalping she had endured. The only hair on her head was in the back. The top of her head no longer existed. Any part of her face that wasn't covered with blood was far whiter than the dress now, blood having drained from her system. I took it all in at a glance.

"Pretty for a squaw, ain't she?" a man in the crowd said.

He said it at the same time I was swinging my rifle full into the plate-glass window, shattering it to pieces. I heard the last of his words as the window broke into a thousand pieces. His comment may have been innocent enough, considering the way the town felt about Indians, but it was definitely the wrong time to say it and the wrong person to say it to. The shattering glass may have surprised them, but not as much as the sight and sound of my Spencer when I spun it around, spotted the man who had spoken, and put a round between his feet, an action which caused him and those near him to quickly move out of the way. Truth be known, I could have killed the bastard! It shocked them even more when I levered another shell into the chamber and pulled back the hammer.

Outrage? Hoss, you never seen anyone as killing mad as I was right then!

"You sanctimonious, hypocritical bastards!" I yelled at them. "Who the hell says she's an *Indian*?"

"The men who put her up there, that's who," one man with guts enough replied. "You're in trouble, mister. You don't go around shooting at innocent people in this city. We won't put up with it."

"Then you ought not to go around killing innocent people!"

"Where do you get off—"

"She wasn't no Indian, you ignorant bastards! Her father was white and her mother a Mexican." That had been the gist of the talk Samuel and Becky and I'd had that one night, them mostly straightening me out about what she was and what she wasn't. Her reason for taking up for the Indians hadn't been because she was one but because she had enjoyed teaching them and found them to be just as good at being humans as the rest of us that walk this earth.

"I was gonna marry her next month," I growled, and took up my rifle again.

"Diah." Billy had a menacing look about him, slowly shaking his head to let me know he didn't want me to get into any more trouble than I likely already was. "You two," he said, pointing to two men on the edge of the crowd, "get inside and take her down. And be careful about it. You," he ordered, pointing to another man, "you find whoever is doing the burying these days and get him over here, and I mean now." The men did as he bade, but I thought I also noticed several others leave the crowd at the same time. They would be back with others to make me pay for the shooting, but I'd be ready.

"No more, Diah. These folks ain't the ones who did it," Billy said.

"Then where'd they go? Where are the ones who did it? Where's Leach?"

"You know, boys, someday I'm going to meet up with you when you aren't in some kind of trouble." Forbush was approaching from the side, as cool and collected as always. He also wore that mischievous grin, as though he was treating it all lightly. At least he wore it until he saw Becky in that window.

Billy gave him a quick going-over of what had taken place in the past few minutes. I had my rifle firmly in hand but was suddenly feeling weak, as though the energy had been sapped from my body. Maybe it was the pain catching up with me, or the cold in the air . . . or knowing that I'd failed to save the woman I loved, and was now coming to the realization that there was nothing I could do about it.

More men were coming toward the crowd now, some with pistols and rifles, all looking like they meant business.

"You men put those guns away," Forbush was saying. "There's been enough bloodshed today."

"And if we don't?" one challenged.

As quick as a flash, the marshal had his Colt out, the pistol an extension of his arm, and aimed it directly at the man who had run off at the mouth.

"If you men don't put those guns away, I'm going to start putting some of you away, and you'll be the first one, George. Now, get out of here or call the bluff."

Trouble was that Glen Forbush wasn't bluffing and they knew it. By the time he'd finished speaking his piece, Billy Breakenridge had a six-gun out and pointed in the general direction of the crowd too. It was simply no contest and the yahoos began to leave. But the rest of the crowd seemed to be out for blood and was just waiting for something to happen.

"You want me to get you out of this, Diah, because I can if you like," Forbush said.

"Don't matter anymore."

"If I get you out, it's on my terms," the marshal said. "Understood?"

I shrugged, still grasping the Spencer.

That was when Forbush hit me hard on the jaw and I felt my knees buckle under me as I blacked out.

Chapter 19

Becky was dressed in that white dress of hers and we were getting ready to walk down the aisle to get married. And we did. But when the preacher started saying his words, they were all about how hateful Indians were. Leach was there and then I looked toward Becky and she wasn't dressed in that pretty wedding dress anymore. Instead, she was as buckskin-clad as any squaw I'd seen at the Sand Creek reservation. She screamed my name as Leach walked up to her, but I couldn't do anything, I couldn't protect her. He had an object in his hand that I couldn't identify and he swung it at Becky. Then her scalp went flying off and there was blood spurting everywhere and I still couldn't do anything! I just stood there. Yet, at the same time, I could feel the pain she was going through. And still I would've traded places with her. But I didn't save her life. I *couldn't* save her life! If only I'd had my rifle, if only I'd had my *Spencer*!

"Easy, now, son," a voice was saying. Then, as an aside, "Lost a good amount of blood, I'd say." To me again, "Your rifle's right over there, son. No need for it now. You just get some rest."

It was the doctor, the same one who had tended to Samuel earlier. Except I wasn't all too sure how much earlier that had been. The last thing I remembered was Forbush hitting me, and if I buckled when he hit me, I had to be weak. Under any other circumstances I would've beat the hell out of the man, for I was bigger than he was.

"Where am I?" I asked. It was dark, so it had to be nighttime. Or was I still dreaming? I could've been dreaming for all I knew. The doctor was ignoring me, as were two other shadowy figures in the room.

"If he doesn't need at least a week's worth of bed rest, I won't bill you for the call," the doctor said. "But right now I'd get some food into him. Food and fresh air are the best healing devices ever created . . . or discovered, I forget which."

As he left, another figure came into view and I focused my eyes on Forbush. After everything that had happened, he was still able to manage a smile.

"You realize, of course, that I'll never be able to deal seconds again," he said. When I squinted at him, he added, "You've got an awful hard jaw, son." Then I remembered.

"Where am I?"

"Turn the light up, Billy. I guess that even in the dark it's hard sometimes for a man to recognize his own room." The light was turned up and I got a full glimpse of Forbush and Breakenridge, both men obviously doing better than me. But it was my room all right. Or maybe I should say it's what passed for my room behind Samuel Botkin's store. "You know, Diah, you can get into more trouble than anyone I know. Except maybe your pa," the marshal added with a smile. "Billy, I'm going to get this loafer some food. Why don't you find the makings and put on some coffee if you will." Then he simply got up and left.

"How's Samuel?" I asked. "Has anyone told him? Does he know?"

Billy smiled. There must've been a whole lot that people thought was funny that day that I just didn't catch hold of. If I remembered that day in November, on the other hand, it wouldn't be for the peace and tranquility in the world that Becky was always talking about. It would be for the horrendous way in which she died. I'd never be able to forget that.

"You know, Diah, for a fella who's been through a lot more than most in just one day, you sure are concerned about a lot of folks other than yourself." If his intention was to remind me of the wound in my leg, it was an effective gesture. I was suddenly quite painfully aware of how my leg felt, although I had to admit that the fresh bandage and proper medical attention did make it a mite more bearable while I was laying flat on my back.

"Samuel's doing fine," he continued. "I think the doctor finally got through to him that the best place for him right now is a bed." Billy chuckled to himself. "Tough old bird, though, I'll give him credit for that."

"Want to tell me what's going on?" I asked. Maybe I was where everyone else thought I should be, but I had ideas of my own about that. "So far you've all been good at dodging the issue. Now let me know what's happening."

I reckon he figured I had to be told sometime or other, but Billy Breakenridge let out a long sigh before he started talking. Seems it had been only about four hours since Forbush had gotten me out of what could have been a tough jam. But Billy had been doing some scouting around of his own in that time and had some interesting news to report.

"That Hank fella you was talking 'bout is the one led those yahoos into Mister Botkin's store and took your woman. The ones Forbush drove out of town that day, it was them that did it. Eight or ten as near as I can find out. Only two of 'em from the original bunch weren't part of it. That sergeant who led 'em and Leach." No, the sergeant wouldn't have been with them, though for the moment only I knew that, for I had killed him there at Sand Creek. But that sergeant had said Leach and the others were going to take care of Becky and that they had. The only problem with the story that Billy was telling was that Leach wasn't there, and that just didn't sound right, as much as the big man laid claim to hating Indians. It must be a mistake. Someone had missed seeing him! Trouble was you couldn't miss seeing Leach, as big as he was. Not hardly.

"Where'd they go?"

Billy shrugged, a puzzled look coming to his face. "I ain't sure, Diah. Some said those boys went about their business like nothing had happened. Way folks feel 'bout injuns hereabouts I reckon that could be true. Others—" He hesitated, them made up his mind. "Well, others ain't saying one way or t'other."

"Don't sound like any of 'em are too scared of getting caught up with by the law." It was a statement of fact, for of late that was how it had been with Chivington's martial law in effect hereabouts.

"Not with some of the celebrating that's been going on tonight. These people are getting a whole different picture painted for 'em of Sand Creek than what you and I saw." There was a bit of sorrow in Billy's voice now. Perhaps he was remembering the atrocities that had happened that morning and would never forget them, in the same way that I would never forget seeing Becky in that store window.

"Ain't it a shame?" I said, my mind sort of wandering.

"What's that?"

"That you can come so close to having everything and then lose it in the bat of an eye." Becky and everything she meant to me were now no more than memories. Truth

to tell, I wasn't too sure I could deal with that. Or wanted
to. I'd never find another girl like Rebecca Botkin, never
know another love like hers, never learn as much from
another person as I had from her. Of that I was certain.
Now it was just like it had been at the start. The only thing
I had left of any importance to me was my Spencer.

"True enough, Diah," Billy said, getting up. "But I
know a hundred men who'd give their life savings to have
for one night what you had with that woman for just a few
months. A shame? Sure, it is. But maybe someday you'll
be able to see how fortunate you really were. Not every
man has someone come along in his life who really cares
for him."

The coffee was ready by the time Forbush returned with
a tray of food. Propped up against the wall, I started in on
the meal, only half-hearing the marshal as he said something about wanting to see me the next morning. When I
looked up next, he was gone.

The doctor was right about the food. It gave me strength,
or maybe only a false feeling of it. Whatever you want to
call it, it was one hell of a lot better than the way I'd felt
before. I told Billy I'd be all right so long as my rifle was
nearby, and asked him to stop by in the morning with some
more ammunition. Convinced that Samuel and I would rest
peacefully that night, he left.

You could call it sneaky if you want, but it accomplished
what I had in mind. I'd been mulling over what Billy had
said about the murderers not being too awful scared or
feeling for their lives, and if they were doing the celebrating tonight that Breakenridge seemed to think they were,
well, so much the better. Me, I was going to put that fear
of God into them at sunrise. What the hell, there wasn't
much left to live for anyway.

"Samuel," I said after taking a good ten minutes to get

down the hallway to his room. He squinted at me in the
dark until I held the lantern up to my face.

"Diah?" He seemed surprised at the sight of me and I
found myself wondering if he hadn't thought I'd up and
deserted him. It seemed likely that he didn't even know I
was down the hall.

"Yeah," I said, sitting down on the edge of his bed
again. My leg wasn't as painful as it had been before, but
that didn't mean it didn't hurt. It hurt like hell!

"No one came back," he said. "You didn't come back.
I must have dozed off."

I took a firm hold of his arm, wanting to steady him but
not sure of my own strength either.

"They killed her, Samuel." His eyes opened wide and
I saw rage begin to build in them. "I found her in that
millinery shop down the street. They scalped her, Samuel.
The bastards *scalped* her."

A man did his grieving in private, but right then I saw
a small man made smaller by the knowledge that his only
daughter was dead. The rage momentarily vanished, but I
knew it would be back, just as mine had returned.

"I'm going to get 'em, Samuel," I said, picking up the
lamp. "In the morning. The sonsabitches ain't getting away
without paying for it first." I was using the Spencer as a
crutch again, holding the lantern in my other hand.

"Diah, you come get me when you're ready," Samuel
said, coughing. "I got nothing better to do." If he made
it out of bed, I knew it would be a miracle. But he'd try,
Samuel would. He was the kind of man you can count on.

"Thanks," was all I said as I made my way down the
hall to my room. I wouldn't sleep that night, for all I had
on my mind was Becky and what I was going to do to
those who'd so cold-bloodedly killed her. I stayed put in
bed as long as I could, resting up my leg, knowing I'd

need every bit of strength in my body come sunup. And all the time there was one thought fixed in my mind.

Whether they knew it or not, when they came after Becky, those murderous bastards bought themselves a one-way ticket to hell. Every last one of them!

Chapter 20

I was cleaning the Spencer for the I-don't-know-how-manyeth time, when Samuel came down the hall. I heard him before I saw him and knew that his cough had gotten worse during the night. He was spitting out gobs of phlegm in thick yellow increments, the way a tobacco chewer would. Except that Samuel Botkin didn't chew. In fact, I had a hunch that if the doctor were to see the fluid he was coughing up, he'd be telling the storekeeper that pneumonia had already set in. Me, I was wondering if I was going to make it myself. If only there was time for a meal. But there wasn't. It was nearing dawn and it was time to roust out the town drunks.

That whole bunch of scum would no doubt have enough money between them to pay for a night's worth of drinking, but few would have any money set aside for a place to sleep it off. That was why I figured to try the livery stable, for that was where most of them would be. Besides, there they'd be close to their horses and most of their worldly possessions in case they had to make a fast getaway. And these types, well, hoss, they didn't have much in the line of worldly possessions and the back door was their favorite entrance and exit. So that's where we were

heading . . . if I could get this tired body of mine to working as well as my rifle was.

"What's the matter, son, can't make it?" Samuel, out
of breath and wheezing when he wasn't coughing, leaned
against the doorway, the sawed-off shotgun in his hand, a
pistol in his waistband.

I grimaced as I tried to take a full step without the use
of the rifle as a crutch; after all, I could hardly use the
Spencer that way and shoot it when a confrontation came
about. The pain was killing me and I had to sit down. In
as bad shape as he was, that didn't elicit much approval
from Samuel, and I wasn't too thrilled about it either.

"She ever tell you what her 'surprise' was?" Samuel
asked.

"Surprise?" Then it registered. I'd forgotten all about
what she'd said before my leaving, about the surprise she'd
have for me when I came back. "Oh. No. She said when
I came back she'd—"

"Diah, she saw the doctor just after you left." Suddenly
I had an uneasy feeling. "She was carrying your child."
Tears welled up in his eyes. "That's what she was so happy
about. She just had to make sure."

That tore it!

"Come on, Samuel," I said, getting up and taking my
first step forward, nearly falling flat on my face as I did
so. "We got us some work to do."

"Yes, Diah, I do believe it's time to collect."

It didn't matter anymore. Nothing mattered anymore.
They'd killed my wife-to-be and my child, and you don't
get away with that in my family. Oh, you can rationalize
the hell out of it, but for all practical purposes, Becky had
been mine from the first day I'd seen her in Kansas and
brought her here. And she'd as much as acknowledged it
by returning my love. And Samuel and Pa hadn't really
had a damn thing to do with it.

If all eight or ten men were there in the livery stable, Samuel and I would have no chance at all of getting back out of there. Like as not, we'd neither one see the sun come to full rise, much less set this day. It was revenge, pure and simple, that kept us going. Me, I was going to kill as many of those sonsabitches as I could before they did the same to me!

It must have been a pathetic sight, the two of us helping each other out that back door of Botkin's and working our way up the alley. A buckboard pulled up before us, but I could barely make out the profile of the man driving it in the predawn light.

"Would you look at that, now?" he chuckled. "The blind leading the blind." Then I knew who it was.

"Forbush, you want to die young?" I growled.

"Seems to me you said that once before, kid." I couldn't quite see it in the gray light of morning, but I knew he was smiling again. "And I'll tell you the same thing now as I did the last time. You look like you're the one who's close to dying."

"Damn it, Forbush, how come you're always so smug about things?" I would've yelled it at him, but it would have sapped my strength.

"Never take life too serious, son. It'll sour you before you become old enough to realize it. Way I see it, you win some and you lose some. The idea is not to lose 'em all.

"Now hoist your keisters up on the tailgate of this thing. You were heading for the livery, weren't you?" Like the gambler he was, he was acting like he held all the cards.

"What makes you think we're going there?" Samuel asked suspiciously. I'd have to agree that I was curious too.

"Come on, fellas," he said as the buckboard slowly moved ahead, "you didn't think I was going to leave you there all by yourselves, did you? Let Hank and his lads take a shot at you? No, I had young Breakenridge sitting out by the counter of your store just in case something happened." He paused and his next words had a guilty sound to them. "I also had him listen in on you two." Another pause. "You know, that boy's going to make a good lawman one of these days."

It was a long ride. Or maybe Forbush was just taking his time to let enough sun rise so we could see who we were shooting at. There was no conversation, and although it was cold and I had no jacket on, I couldn't really feel it. My mind had one sole thought, one lone purpose, and that was killing.

"You could at least tell me you're grateful, you know," Forbush said as we neared the livery. "I was holding four kings with an ace kicker when Billy came and got me. You wouldn't believe the money that was in the pot either!"

"What the hell did you come for, then?" Samuel sounded mad, as though he'd had enough of the marshal's easygoing manner too.

"Hell, someone's got to keep you from getting killed. Besides, that's what they pay me for, remember? Ain't that going to make some headline in the paper? 'MARSHAL FINALLY DOES HIS JOB.' Lordy, will they have fun with that."

He was all too carefree about the whole matter, especially about the possibility of getting killed, which was quite real. When we pulled up in front of the livery, I decided it was time for some straight answers.

"I want to know the real reason, Glen." It was the first time I'd called him by his first name. Strange how little things like that strike you when you're about to go through hell. "And this time deal it from the top of the deck."

"You want the *real* reason, Diah? All right. About twenty years ago I knew a young lady just like your Becky. Just like you, I lost her. It was a stray bullet that killed her. I never fell in love again. Swore to myself that I wouldn't. That's why it made me feel good about you and Becky getting engaged. That's why I said I'd pay for the wedding." The light was bright enough for me to see his face now, and it was dead serious. "There's also the fact that I hate to see people like this get away with murder."

Samuel said nothing but I nodded, letting him know that I understood. Suddenly, I had an urge when all this was over to get to know Glen Forbush better. Man wasn't half bad.

"Samuel, why don't you keep watch on the side of the livery," Forbush said. "I've got a notion these bastards are going to be as sneaky as they can." Samuel moved off to the side, as he was told. "Diah, you keep an eye on the roof and that second-story hayloft. That long gun of yours ought to come in handy there."

"And what are you going to be doing?"

He thumbed the tin star.

"I have the dubious honor of rousting these birds and notifying them they're headed for jail."

He started toward the big building without waiting for a comment, but he didn't have to go far. The doors to the hayloft and the front of the livery opened, almost at the same instant. There looked to be only one man in the loft, but the four who walked through the ground-floor entrance were definitely more than Glen Forbush could take on at one time.

"Time to decide, boys," the marshal said, nary a nervous twitch in his voice. Cool as a cucumber, as Pa would put it. "You either go to jail or go to hell, and to tell you the truth, I don't give a damn which."

Two of them made the mistake of looking at each other in pure amazement before going for their guns, and I'm here to tell you that it was all the edge Forbush needed. Hoss, you never seen four men die so fast in so short a time! Their pistols hadn't even cleared leather before he plugged them one shot each and they were taking the short route to hell before they hit the ground.

I shot the one in the hayloft before he could take aim. If he'd had a six-gun, he might have killed the marshal, like he obviously planned, but he had a rifle and it was taking him time to get a good position. Me, I had him in my sights all the time and blew his brains out the minute he made the first wrong move.

Five down, and less than fifteen seconds had passed.

Then all hell broke loose. Samuel had been watching what Forbush had accomplished, totally forgetting what he was supposed to be doing himself. That accounted for the shot he took in the side while two more of the bastards moved up alongside the livery—just like Forbush had said they would. Samuel was down now but the two men didn't get past him. Like I said, you could count on Samuel. Each one of them took a barrel of buckshot in the gut as they tried to rush past Botkin to Forbush. Tossing the shotgun aside, Samuel pulled out his pistol and propped himself up far enough to be able to shoot both men in the head. Then another shot rang out and Samuel's body slammed back onto the ground. He was dead and it was my fault because the shot had come from the hayloft.

The rifleman was taking a second aim, going for Forbush, when I killed him.

"Sonofabitch!" I said, leaving the cover of the buckboard. I was mad, as angry at myself as I was at any of the rest of them. That was when another of them came from the far side of the barn and caught Forbush off guard. He took the bullet in the midsection and fell to the ground. I snapped off a shot at the assailant, and thought I hit him in the arm, although he managed to disappear behind the barn.

Samuel was dead, his body lifeless, but for the moment

the shooting had stopped and I said a silent prayer of thanks to whoever it is that listens to them that I was still alive and hadn't been hit. I made my way to Forbush and knelt down beside him.

"See, kid, told you," he coughed, still smiling. "You win some and you lose some."

"Sure, Glen. Let me get a doctor. You're gonna be fine."

He shook his head. "I'm the gambler, remember. Don't you think I know the odds?" Then he paused, as though thinking some deep thought. "Can't understand where they were."

"Who?"

A look of surprise came to his face then, the kind you expect to see on a dying man when he knows the end is near. But it wasn't that kind of surprise. He was looking past me and I turned to see the ugly, greedy, meaner-than-hell face of Hank. He had a gun out and was cocking it when a bullet from Forbush's sleeve gun went through his heart and he fell, dead.

"Told you I'd kill you on sight." Glen Forbush had that smug little grin on his face when he said it. He died that way.

I was getting damn tired of surprises, especially the kind that killed. The thought that I still hadn't seen Leach was crossing my mind as I levered another round into my Spencer and struggled to get to my feet in case the rest of Hank's crowd hadn't had the good sense to get the hell out of there.

They hadn't.

Three of them came into view at once, two from the side of the livery, the other from inside. But none of them came even close to looking like Leach. They all had guns and they were all going to use them—on me.

I shot the one standing in the doorway, but that was the

end of the ball for me. I was levering another shell into the
Spencer, when the pair who'd rounded the corner started
throwing lead at me. One slug yanked at my shoulder,
spinning me partway around and causing me to trip over
Forbush's body, which likely saved my life.

What followed next was a blaze of gunfire that I only
heard, none of which hit me, which seemed miraculous at
the time. But I knew it wasn't over, knew that until I'd
found Leach, I'd always be watching my back. When the
gunfire subsided, I got up the strength to push myself up
and over with my one good arm. I still had the Spencer in
the other hand, which is when it happened.

Walking toward me was Leach, looking as mean as always, gun in hand. I knew he'd finally come to kill me,
knew I had one last chance to get him before he got me. I
swung the rifle around, figuring I'd pot-shot him if I could.
But he kicked the rifle out of my hand and just stood there
holding the gun in his hand, looking like he was going to
kill me.

Maybe it was all that blood I felt coming out of me, or
the knowledge that I was about to die and finally meet my
Maker. Whatever it was it had an effect on me. Leach was
still standing there, deciding whether or not he was going
to kill me, when I passed out.

Chapter 21

Leach never did kill me. Fact is, he saved my life.

It was his guns that had done most of the shooting that day after I'd been put out of business my own self. It was Leach who'd stepped in and killed the last two tough guns when they were readying to do me in permanent. I reckon I'd been getting weaker and dizzier as the whole ordeal had gone on, for one of the reasons he kicked the rifle from my hand was that I'd jammed it into some mud when I'd fallen over Forbush's body. If I'd fired that gun with the barrel plugged up like it was, why, I'd have had all sorts of metal peeling back into my face and just plain pushing my own brains out. So I didn't cuss all that much when I found out that Leach had near busted a couple of my fingers.

I spent at least two weeks in bed before I even attempted to take another look at the outside world. I had visits from a lot of folks, one of them a businessman who said he had an interest in buying the Botkin General Store. He offered a price that sounded like a good one and said it would take as long as it took me to heal to get all of his paperwork done. So when I got up and around again, we finished up the deal. I had him make a check out to that Aunt Louise

159

that Becky had stayed with in St. Louis, figuring she'd know who ought to get it.

I also had some visits from Leach, the hardest one being the first.

"I loved her just as much as you did, Hooker," he said that first time when we got around to discussing Becky. It was a hard thing for him to say, I think. "Only I knew she wouldn't have me, so I backed off when she made it clear it was you she favored.

"There was times you was gone that I talked with her when no one else seen us." Hearing it made me mad at first and I wanted him to leave, but he held up his hand, knowing how I felt. "Toward the end there she said she was going to tell you 'bout it as a surprise."

"A surprise?" This didn't make sense, considering what Samuel had said before the shootout, none at all. I guess not even he'd known about the meetings between Becky and Leach. "What was the surprise?"

He blushed, glancing around as though anyone hearing our conversation would purely embarrass him.

"She had a good head on her shoulders, Miss Becky did. She told me 'bout how she'd taught Indians and how they wasn't savages after all. I reckon you could say she taught me how to have a better respect for humans, no matter where they come from, or which side of the fightin' they're on. He smiled briefly, then gave me a serious look. "But if you ever tell anyone that, I'll bust up whatever bones in your body ain't hurting right now."

I smiled. "It's a deal, Leach. Your secret is safe with me."

So that was the "surprise" Becky had been planning. She was going to let me know she'd converted Leach, probably the biggest and toughest Indian hater she had ever met. Yes, I suppose that would have been a surprise. I know it was then, when the big man told me himself.

By the time I got to hobbling around, Christmas had come and gone and so had the praise for Chivington and his men. More and more the truth was coming out about how they had massacred the Cheyenne and Arapahoe, who had agreed upon a peace treaty and were doing nothing more than waiting for its approval when the "Fighting Parson" swept down on them with a killing vengeance.

"Worst thing to happen since the Council House Fight," I said to Leach one day. But he'd never heard of it, so I had to explain to him what Pa had told us youngsters some years back. "Army tried making peace with the Comanches back in the spring of 'Forty, inviting their chiefs to come in to San Antonio. The Comanche took 'em up on it . . . could've made peace too. But the white man broke his word and that Council House Fight, well, it was sort of a smaller version of what happened at Sand Creek. Comanches ain't made a treaty yet, likely won't.

"Same thing is gonna happen here, Leach. I'd wager you'll see more tribes who at one time would've fought one another making peace with each other for the sole purpose of ridding us whites from their land. And it's all because of Chivington and his men."

"Could be right, Hooker," the big man replied. "I been hearing 'bout some Cheyenne activity up in the Nebraska Territory. Could be."

I thought a lot about Becky and Samuel and Glen Forbush in that time too. I'd miss them all, but Becky the most. There was still a lot of pain to deal with that would be worse than that caused by any arrow or bullet I'd ever taken, pain that would take longer to heal than my wounds. After a while I decided that the doctor who had worked on Samuel and me was right. Food and fresh air were about the best healing sources a body could have. I'd had my fill of decent food while I recovered. Now, well, maybe it was

time to move on. Besides, there was that check I had to
get to Becky's Aunt Louise in St. Louis.

The morning I was getting ready to leave I met Leach
coming out of the bar he so often frequented. There was
fire in his eyes that said there was a fight coming. In fact,
the handful of men who scattered from the saloon had the
same look.

"You were right, Diah," he said excitedly. It was the
first time he'd called me by my first name. "Them Cheyenne up Nebraska way declared all-out war! Hurry up! You
can ride with us!"

"No thanks," I said. "I think I'll sit this one out. I'd
better get myself healed up proper before I go out to do
any more fighting."

At first he got that same old bullheaded look on his face
that said he wanted things his way, but then it changed
some and he simply stuck out his paw. "Sure, I understand. You take care of yourself."

I took his hand, thinking it was likely the first time I'd
shaken it. It was hard to believe that I'd actually learned
to get along with the man. And now both of us were leaving. Still, a man's got his curiosity.

"Leach," I said as he mounted up.

"Yeah."

"What's your first name?"

"Oh, no. I ain't telling that! You think I want to ruin
my reputation?" He said it half in jest, half seriously as
he gave me an informal salute before riding off.

Inside the saloon I had one last beer, a salute to an old
friend I'd gotten to know too late.

"How's business, Ben?" I asked the burly bartender.

"Kinda slacked off some recently." He toweled another
shot glass for something to do. "I sure will miss Marshal
Forbush," he added in a sad tone. "He knew how to pack
'em in. Why, do you know that he had those games a-

going—'' He stopped quickly, a nervous, surprised look coming to his face. "Oh, lordy." Then he disappeared for a minute, like a mother hen looking for a missing chick. "Here," he said when he returned, thrusting a thick envelope into my hands. "He said to give this to you when you come around."

"I don't understand."

"Well, that morning that everything happened, Marshal Forbush had stayed here all night playing poker. Yes, sir. Didn't stop until the Breakenridge boy come to get him. Then he called me over and told me to finish playing out his hand, just like he always did if he had to leave sudden like. Wrote himself out a quick letter, gave it to me, and said to put his winnings in it if his hand won. Do you know what he—"

"I'll bet it was four kings with an ace kicker," I said.

"Yes, but how did you—"

"He told me."

"Well, I'll be," he said in amazement, although I don't know what it was about.

I opened the envelope and pulled out a folded piece of paper.

Diah,
  You were right about me not paying you enough for what you did for me, so whatever is enclosed is yours. Maybe it'll help get you started in some other line of work, although I know it could never ease the pain.
  But don't let the pain follow you through life like it did me. It'll make you miserable and you'll regret it when you're old enough to know better. You see, there was once a girl I knew. But that's a whole 'nother canyon.
  One other thing. If you're holding kings with an ace kicker, bet the ranch! I just did. The pity is that I'll never know whether I won or not.

It was signed in Glen Forbush's own hand.

"You won, Glen," I said to myself, "in more ways than one."

"Pardon?"

"Oh, nothing, Ben. Say, how much is in here?" There was a hell of a lot of money by the looks of it.

"Five thousand four hundred and fifty dollars," Ben said proudly. "Counted it myself."

I didn't know what in the hell I'd do with all that much money, but for starters I dug through the bills until I found fifty dollars worth. Then I passed it across the bar to Ben, "Here, buy the house a few drinks."

He seemed surprised, but then, there was a lot of that going around these days. "But, what will I tell 'em? How do I explain it?"

I grinned. "Tell 'em Glen Forbush always buys the last round. Yeah, Ben, tell 'em that."

I left then, taking my time riding out of Denver. There were a lot of memories there, but I'd as soon forget most of them. I found myself wondering, instead, if there was any truth to the letter I'd just read. Would I ever really find another woman like Rebecca Botkin in my lifetime?

Or a friend like Glen Forbush?

About the Author

Jim Miller began his writing career at the age of ten when his uncle presented him with his first Zane Grey novel. A direct descendant of Leif Erickson and Eric the Red, and a thirteen-year Army veteran, Mr. Miller boasts that stories of adventure flow naturally in his blood. His novels to date include SUNSETS, the six books in the Colt Revolver series: GONE TO TEXAS, COMANCHE TRAIL, WAR CLOUDS, RIDING SHOTGUN, ORPHANS PREFERRED and CAMPAIGNING, and Long Guns novels THE BIG FIFTY, MISTER HENRY, and SPENCER'S REVENGE.

When not busy writing about the future exploits of the Hooker men, Mr. Miller spends his time ensconced in his two-thousand-volume library filled mostly with history texts on the Old West. He lives in Aurora, Colorado, with his wife Joan and their two children.

JIM MILLER'S
SHARP-SHOOTIN'
ST⊚RIES
O' THE WAYS
O' THE WEST!!